HORRORS:
Real,
Imagined,
& Deadly

HORRORS:
Real,
Imagined,
& Deadly

EDITED BY MATT SINCLAIR

TABLE OF CONTENTS

Introduction: Secret Fears

What are you afraid of? What causes the hair on your neck to stand up? Was there a room in your childhood home that always gave you the creeps? Are there personal demons you've never quite exorcised?

Fear is personal. I've known many who claim to be fearless. I think they lie. If I were evil, I would explore their personal fears to find out if I'm right. But I'm not that evil. I freely admit that I have fears. Heights for one, though it's more about having nothing above me than peering down at a depth that would likely see my demise if I fell. I wonder what my fear might mean; I hope it simply implies that I'm uncomfortable without having a higher goal to reach for. Lord knows I haven't reached all my goals.

Of course, there are also fears we share with no one. Perhaps yours is a fear of dying alone, friendless and forgotten—or maybe it's just death itself. Then again, maybe you wear a mask and it's a fear that your true nature will be revealed, whatever that might be. What horrifies us might be nothing to someone else. I have a friend I would trust with my life, but she wouldn't be caught dead driving in New York City, while I might not so much as lock the doors. And I couldn't tell you how many friends I have who love to talk about their favorite horror stories but fail to see the monsters in their own lives. That's scary in itself.

I believe, dear readers, you will find several stories in our collection that will make you keep a light on when you go to bed. Ideally, each one would do so. But as I said, horror is personal. And many fears are secret.

We lead off with a story from Precy Larkins, who imagines a "Dream House" that would leave Barbie and Ken petrified. In "Blood and Ink," the irrepressible Mindy McGinnis explores the anguished musings of a librarian keeping her debilitating sickness a secret. Charlee Vale's "The Ice Tree" shows that sometimes curiosity leads to tragedy. Then there's "The Sound of the Chain" by R.S. Mellette, which is not your typical horror story, but anyone who appreciates the pursuit of knowledge will recognize the specters within the tale.

If you enjoyed these stories, please let us know. Send me an email at matt@elephantsbookshelfpress.com. I'd love to know what you think about Real, Imagined, and Deadly. And visit us on Facebook, where we promise not to be too scary. As any herd of elephants knows, there's safety in numbers.

—Matt Sinclair

THE DREAM HOUSE
Precy Larkins

*I*T'LL BE ALL RIGHT, MRS. PARKER. *We won't give up hope. The tests were inconclusive.* Anna's hand clenched tighter around the paisley-patterned mug someone gifted her and Bradley last Christmas. She looked down at the kitchen table, at the crumbs dotting the wooden surface, at the honey lemon-flavored tea puddle threatening to spill over the edge.

Inconclusive. Anna hated the word. It sounded too much like failure.

She glanced at the ticking wall clock. Five a.m. *Five?* An hour had gone by without her notice? Her tea was cold and useless. She got up, chair legs scraping shrilly through the morning quiet, and dumped her drink in the sink, her thoughts returning once more to her doctor appointment yesterday.

There are still options, the gynecologist had said. What she heard instead was: We're running out of options.

Bradley didn't come with her to the clinic. He stopped going after a year of failed treatments, stopped hoping after the miscarriage that brought the chill to their bedroom. Still, she wished he had come, if only to hold her hand.

Rain softly knocked on the roof of their apartment complex. For a moment she wondered if it was the pitter-patter that woke her up. But no, it was a dream. The same one recurring since the night she married Bradley.

She should go back to bed. Try to sleep.

Try to catch remnants of her dream.

Anna shrugged out of her robe. She rolled over to her husband's side and wrapped an arm around his waist. He didn't stir. The faint morning light seeped through the gauze curtains on their window, and Anna pulled the covers around her to keep warm. She shivered, rubbing her icy feet together. But sleep refused to visit her and Bradley began to snore.

She closed her eyes and breathed in the stale bedroom air, the smell of threadbare carpeting down the hallway, the musky odor of a place that had seen too many people, too many years.

"I want my own place," she whispered. And the house in her dream began to take shape. Anna pulled out the sketchpad she kept hidden within the nightstand and started sketching.

Bradley was late. Anna sat in her car, afraid to come out and meet the realtor by herself. She already knew she hated *this* house. It wasn't the one. Not the house she dreamed of night after night. Not the house that comforted her in dreams, when reality sometimes meant cold sheets on the other side of the bed. This house had no graying roof shingles, no French windows, and no lovely terrace. Instead, a tiny, nondescript porch led to an ugly black door, most likely made of fiberboard—not real wood.

Her house would have stairs that seemed to go on forever. She could see it now—the smooth banisters with carved balustrades, the high ceilings, mosaic tiles on the kitchen floor depicting roses, and the massive wooden mantel above the fireplace. It would have five rooms, one of them a nursery with pastel walls. Her favorite would be the master bedroom with its massive canopy bed furnished with silk curtains hanging off its posts. A true luxury, and Anna blushed at the thought of making love on such a bed.

Someone rapped at her window, and Anna jumped. It was only her husband, with his devilish smile and pale blue eyes.

"Hey, baby," Bradley said as she got out of her old Volkswagen. "Sorry to keep you waiting. You should have gone inside and checked out the rooms with Miss Farrell instead of braving the cold out here." He pecked her on the cheek. Anna wrapped her scarf tighter around her neck.

"I don't think this is the one."

"What's that? But you haven't even been inside. You should—"

Anna shook her head. "No. I know this isn't our house."

Bradley sighed and ran his fingers over his slightly overgrown hair. "Baby, we're not having this conversation again."

Anna bit her lip, a habit she'd acquired of late. It took over the endless pacing she'd been doing most nights, waiting for Bradley to come home. But once, when she was deep in thought and didn't hear him come in, he'd caught her pacing the length of their living room, which wasn't very long or very far. Bradley's raised eyebrow had made her quit abusing the carpet to abuse her lips instead.

"Anna?"

"No." She didn't want to live in the apartment any more than he did, but this didn't feel right. "No."

Bradley's eyes turned gray…something that Anna had never seen before in all the years of their married life. *Must be a trick of the light.* The skies were gray, after all. A spring day still caged in winter's grip.

"You're being unreasonable, you know that?" Bradley's words came out harsh and sharp. Hot needle tears pricked Anna's eyes. She slid back into the driver's seat, her fingers fumbling to turn the key in the ignition. Her husband backed away from her car as the engine roared to life, and Anna only had a second to glimpse the frown on Bradley's face.

"Screw you," she muttered under her breath as she pulled onto the street. She wasn't *delusional*. Still, the downward curl of his lips, his glaring eyes, the tone of his voice…they were new to her and spoke of his obvious disdain for her dream. "Screw. You."

She blinked back the tears in time to see the traffic light turning red. She could make for the highway and go home, back to the rat hole she despised. Or she could keep driving to who knew where. A little girl's face appeared in her periphery—a child staring at her from the corner of the street. Anna leaned forward, her chin almost touching the steering wheel. The girl had her eyes. A murky green pair dotted with brown hues. How she could tell from this distance she didn't know, but Anna knew they were *her* eyes.

Someone honked behind her. Anna signaled right and turned onto the dirt road, her gaze never wavering from the girl's face. She thought she saw a smile, but then she checked her rearview mirror—one second, two—and the girl was gone.

She probably ran off to hide behind the bushes. I can't believe her parents would let her play alone, and so close to the street! Anna's stomach twisted in its familiar ache and longing for one of her own. Her gynecologist had delivered unpromising news, but he'd also mentioned hope…and more future tests. How long had it been? How long had they tried? Too many years of pain and longing had blurred together, and only the faint grooves on her brow spoke of the count. No matter. Once they found her house, everything would fall into place. She was certain. Anna touched her flat belly with her free hand, imagining it to be round and ripe. A watermelon full of swollen promises and tiny giggles and soft, tickly toes. She smiled.

She followed the curve of the road, hardly glancing at the trees lining up the path like giant sentinels guarding a secret. Anna had never been to this part of the town, and yet, there was something familiar about its ruggedness and the way the leafy bowers waved her toward her destination. She rolled down her window, and the chilly wind swooped in to sting her cheeks. A rusty metal arrow sign squeaked, swiveling on its screw before pointing to a narrower path down a fork in the road. *Eidolene Drive.* What a strange name! Anna craned her neck to see where it ended, but copses of firs and pine trees covered the rest of the lane from her sight. She stepped on the brakes as she came to the mouth of the dirt road.

This is crazy, and it's probably private property. I should get back to Bradley. Anna sighed, reaching for the gear shift. Getting back to Bradley meant silence and excuses to be doing something else…something other than figuring out what had gone wrong between them. If only they had a child, if only they had the right house. Things would be different, would be right. She just knew it.

Feathery snowflakes floated through her open window. "Oh, great. It's the middle of April, for crying out loud."

The engine stalled. Anna turned off the ignition. "Damn old junk!" She slapped the steering wheel, accidentally beeping the horn. Between the foliage and tree trunks closely huddled together, a face peered out to look at her.

Anna started. "Oh, geez, what the hell?"

It was the little girl. Her grass-stained dress had tears along the hem, and her feet were bare and covered in grime. With one hand, she clutched a headless doll to her thin chest. Her hair, a dirty red, curled around her shoulders. For someone so young, her face looked oddly...*aged*. And knowing. As if she'd already seen the world a thousand times over, her eyes holding secrets behind their long dark lashes.

Anna opened her car door a crack. The girl did not stir but continued to stare at her, unblinking.

"Hello?" she called out.

Nothing. No movement. The girl's face was like chiseled stone, hard and edged...and unnerving.

"Are you lost? Where do you live?" Anna carefully slid out of her car, not wanting to scare the child away. "Do you need help? It's okay, I won't hurt you." She held out a hand.

The girl's face contorted briefly—her eyes narrowing into slits. She let out an angry hiss and darted back toward the wooded cluster. Anna staggered backwards, her heart thumping. She wiped her clammy hands on her faded jeans. *What the hell was that about?*

Snow fell like soft whispers against her skin. Anna grabbed her purse from the passenger seat and rummaged inside for her cell phone. The battery was dead. She'd forgotten to charge it last night.

"Oh, crap," she blurted, pressing the lock button on her car key. She'd have to find a phone somewhere to call Bradley. Anna shook off the white flakes from her leather boots and began walking down Eidolene Drive.

It really was a beautiful path, and she could almost imagine the trees in their full glory once summer came. The thought made her calm. She was a country girl at heart.

Up ahead, clipped hedges curved along the road—a sign of civilization! Anna sprinted toward the carefully trimmed bushes barely covering a brick wall. A black wrought-iron gate appeared at the end of the wall…and *there*. It was Anna's house.

Her dream home. Every line and tile and stone an exact replica of her early morning sketches. She couldn't believe it. Anna gripped the iron rails on the gate, and with an ear-splitting squeak, the hinges moved. She stepped back, half-expecting someone—anyone—to accost her for trespassing. But there was only dead silence, and even the snow halted its assault.

She entered.

"Hello?" Her voice sounded small, weak. The air felt too thick to breathe. A bird cawed somewhere over the woods surrounding the enclosure. Anna's boots crunched on the unpaved driveway. A light lit up in one of the upstairs rooms. She knew it was the nursery, which she'd often visited in her dreams, running her hand along the crib that would soon be there.

It was *her* house! Laughter bubbled in her chest, her throat, until she could no longer hold it in. There was the terrace where she would place a rocker, the bold red door with its brass knocker, the gray roof shingles, and the kitchen window where the sink would be situated. Anna wrapped her arms around herself and took a spin.

An old man shuffled in from the side of the house and stopped. His eyes bulged, jaw slacking open. The gardening hoe he held in one hand fell with a clang against the terrace post.

"Oh, I'm so sorry. I didn't mean—the gate was open. I didn't know—" Anna wrung her hands together. "Look, I'm really sorry…"

The man gave a yelp, turned around, and ran out of her view. Anna chewed her bottom lip before calling out. "Hey, wait, I just want to know who lives here!"

Silence. It was as if the man never appeared. If it weren't for the hoe still lying crooked among the weeds growing near the terrace steps, Anna would have thought she imagined the old gardener into existence. What was his deal, anyway? Anna hesitated by the massive front door, her trembling fingers hovering above the round brass knob. It was like déjà vu. She remembered the feel of the knob in her hand, as if she had gripped it multiple times over multiple years. A recorder of her comings and goings. But that was impossible, wasn't it? This was the first time she'd ever been here.

The door opened easily, hardly creaking a protest against her, the trespasser. She didn't even think of knocking. The thought of getting arrested seemed laughable. Anna felt as though the house wanted her to come in, to swallow her and satiate its hunger, its longing. Welcoming back its rightful owner. A rush of feeling overwhelmed Anna as her boots clacked on the wooden floor. This really was her house! Every nook and cranny as familiar as the lines on her palm. There was the porcelain vase filled with lilies on top of the coffee table. The Oriental rug with its vivid hues of red and yellow. And look! Here was the kitchen window where she'd chopped vegetables by the sink, occasionally glancing out to the yard to watch the twirl of pink cotton fabric going round and round…accompanied by high-pitched laughter. *Ring around the rosy, a pocketful of posies… Mama, watch me!*

Mama. Someone had once called her *mama.*

Anna's grip on the sink slipped. This was insane. Bradley was right—she was delusional. Losing her mind over a dream. Maybe she imagined the girl because…because she wanted one. Anna clutched her stomach. Maybe this house was featured in one of those Home and Lifestyle magazines gathering dust at the gynecologist's office, and she must had seen it then. Hence, the familiarity. It was possible, and the most logical explanation.

Yes, of course. That must be it.

Then why did her hand throb, remembering the slice of a knife against her skin? Why—

"Mama?"

Anna spun around at the sound of the girl's voice. She stood on top of the stairs, just across the hallway, a miniature figure in white and pink. Immaculate red curls held together by a single ribbon, her feet encased in plain white socks, delicate hands clutching a doll with its head intact. She was, no doubt, the girl Anna saw earlier by the street, albeit cleaned up and given a new doll to play with.

"Mama?"

"I'm not," Anna said, her breath catching in her throat. "I'm not your mother. Sorry." But even as she said the words, the girl's eyes held the truth. Anna choked back a tear. There was no mistaking the resemblance.

"Mama? Did you come to stay with me?"

Anna nodded, her face wet now. Fingers splayed flat on her stomach. Her body trembled.

"For ever and ever?"

Anna whispered *yes*. She held out her arms.

The girl did not move. "Promise?"

"I…I will never leave you." As soon as Anna said it, she knew it was a mistake. She covered her mouth with her hands, but there was no going back and the girl knew this, a sly grin slowly crept across her impish face.

The stairs creaked. The girl was coming down. Anna tried to make her feet move toward the door, but they wouldn't budge. *Too late! Too late!* the walls around her seemed to cry.

The change was subtle, but it was there all the same. First, the ribbon slithered down the girl's shoulders, freeing the mass of curls, which were matted underneath with greenish-black mold and something dark and much more sinister. Anna knew what it was but she refused to believe it. The girl's smile did not leave her face, a cross between a smirk and a sneer. With each step, her dress became filthier, the hem unraveling in places.

Her socks crumbled away like dust, revealing bare feet splattered with mud.

"Mama, you came back for me. I've been so lonely without you." The girl held out her arms, her pale skin speckled with purple bruises and numerous cuts. A maggot wriggled out of a swollen, festering wound, and dropped onto the floor by Anna's feet. Anna shrieked but she couldn't move away. There was no strength left in her.

"Mama, why didn't you help me? I've been hurting for a very long time." A thin, red choker appeared on the girl's neck. It grew and widened, until Anna realized it was blood swelling, blood gushing from the razor-thin cut embracing the girl's swan-like neck. A macabre smile made of scarlet and horror to match the one glued on her face. The girl gripped Anna's arms, and whispered, "You will stay with me forever."

Anna screamed.

The moon hid its face behind black clouds so that only the flashing red and blue lights could be seen down Eidolene Drive. Yellow police tapes sectioned off a part of the path where Anna's car was found. Hours of snow had masked Anna's footprints, but it didn't matter. They knew she had gone to the house. What they didn't know was where she went after the old gardener saw her.

"I tell ya, I ain't going back in there," the gardener said, his callused hands trembling on his lap. "I done nothing wrong, and you can't make me go back in there. That there house is haunted, don't you know? Fifty years ago it was the scene of a violent crime, it was. Murder and suicide, so I been told."

Detective Lund ushered in Bradley, pushing him toward the old man. "Look here, Mister—"

"Carl. The name's Carl."

"This is the lady's husband. Tell him what you saw again. Tell him what happened to his wife."

The gardener started, then shuddered. As if he'd recognized Bradley, though they'd never met before. His dark eyes clouded, silently appraising, before his next words rushed out in a huff of exasperation. "I already told you lot, didn't I? I didn't do nothing. I didn't see much. She was there, and then she wasn't."

Bradley held up a picture of Anna. "You're sure this was her?"

"Yes, sir, I'm sure of it," the old man said slowly. "See, you won't believe me, but I've seen her walking around the house every night. A specter. A ghost. And I ain't the only one—Mrs. Fieldings, she's the cleaning lady, comes once a month to get the house in order, see. Mrs. Fieldings had seen her, too, when she was working late. Never came back, did she? Spooked her, that's what. Even though them owners pay us plenty enough to keep the house and grounds in order, though they never come here so I don't know what for, but I ain't complaining on account of I get good money for it. The lady—your wife, sir, if you say so—haunts the house most nights. Sometimes I seen her walking outside, looking at that there house, like she was inspecting or something. But most nights, she's up in the nursery—that room upstairs that always has a light on, though there ain't nobody there."

"This is lunacy," said Bradley, balling his hands into fists.

"Just hear him out." The detective nodded at Carl to continue.

"I tell ya, I haven't had a drop to drink in me for years, so I'm sober as can be. I know what I saw, and I know she wasn't alive. Why, she passed through walls! But she'd only ever come out at night. Today was the first time I saw her in daylight, as clear as I see you now, and it was the first time she'd talked to anybody, too. Look, I hightailed it outta there as fast as I could, and dunno why you're still keeping me here, but I betcha if you search the house tonight you'll meet her wandering the hallways in the moonlight."

Detective Lund shook his head. "We found nothing. Except for this." He held out a ragged, headless doll, its clothes stained dark with decades-old blood. Carl's eyes widened but he didn't say anything.

"Detective, can I go? To the house, I mean. I just want to make sure," Bradley asked. He pulled out a sketchpad from his briefcase and flipped it open, revealing pages and pages of detailed drawings.

Detective Lund nodded. As they strode toward the house, the gardener called out.

"You were there, too." He pointed to Bradley. "I seen you before. With her."

Through the nursery window, Anna watched the men enter the courtyard. Her heart skipped at the sight of Bradley, but hope died down quickly. He wouldn't see her, wouldn't hear her. Not yet, anyway. It wasn't time.

"Mama?"

"He'll come around, my darling. He will." The girl was nestled in her lap. Anna stroked the girl's curls, her fingers getting tangled in the blood-soaked hair. She got what she wanted, didn't she? Her dream had come true, and everything would finally be all right.

Anna smiled. She was home.

BLOOD AND INK
Mindy McGinnis

TAKING A BOTTLE OF JAMESON to work wasn't exactly smiled upon in the public schools, but Kitty wasn't thrilled about the penises sketched into her big dictionary and figured a slug or two might give her patience. No one had told her when she got her Masters in Library Science that part of her job description would involve a big pink eraser and eradicating the self-aggrandizements of prepubescents.

The previous librarian had lacked either the interest in a thirty-pound book or the strength to move it, and Kitty's own energy was being eaten away by the cancerous cells she kept secret from her co-workers. So the dictionary remained tucked in the shadowy corner, the victim of giggles and any passerby with a pencil.

Kitty sat at the circulation desk, huddled defensively against the hormones of the teens and baking in her own chemo-soaked aura, now lightly accented with Irish whiskey. The day slipped by, students and staff left the building. The motion sensor lights went out as she lost herself in the call of research: finding the paper trails of her Gaelic ancestors. The dead were so much more interesting than the living, especially now that she had a deadline to become one.

They whirled around her, speaking a language she'd tried to learn but failed as her mind slipped away, fueled now by chemicals and alcohol instead of blood. Her once stark, ordered handwriting had begun to slant in different directions and she let it go, intrigued by the new look of her letters and the tiny symbols she'd begun to ink in the margins.

The chaos in her head stood in direct contrast to the neatly ordered files on her laptop, the censuses, birth and death records, marriages and pictures of tombstones that made her ancestors' voices seem all the louder in her skull, her handwriting increasingly less like her own. So many records had been lost to fire. More than a few of her ancestors, too.

Around three in the morning she lost the battle with vertigo and fell. The whiskey bottle smashed beneath her clawed hand and drove glass slivers into her palm, red blood mixing with black ink on her fingertips. The cacophony stopped, the present and the past now at peace with each other as she made her way to the shadowy corner with an eraser in hand, the fumes of Irish whiskey mixed with the faintest, inexplicable whiff of smoke.

And all around the county, sleeping boys shifted in their sleep as they were suddenly, painlessly, castrated.

THE SOUND OF THE CHAIN
R.S. Mellette

THERE'S SOMETHING UNIQUE about the sound of a chain. Each link, individually so delicate, makes a harmless, charming ting; but together, when slammed on a heavy wooden table as Aaron had just done, they combine into a dangerous thud.

The old man didn't say anything. His intense focus and dramatic chain hushed the twenty or so men in the room. Their ages varied from sixteen to sixty, but their faces held the same, hesitant expression. Their hesitation came from not knowing. They didn't know how they were going to pay their bills. They didn't know where their next meal would come from. The men who were fathers didn't know what to say to their hungry kids. The men who were sons didn't know how to handle the shame of their fathers. Hard times had hit everyone, but these men had been hit harder than most and they didn't know why.

The only thing they did know—those responsible for their ruined lives were about to get what they deserved. The hesitation was about to end. The uncertainty was over. These men stood on the brink of action.

John stepped up next to the old man. If a vote were taken, John would have been elected leader. In his thirties, he had yet to lose his junior college football physique. He was the only one of the mob to have ventured beyond high school. Then he blew out his knee and came back home to assume the mantle of town hero—a job in title only. "It's come to this, my friends. We know they're out there. We know they've been living among us for far too long. We know what they've done. They've ruined this country. We know what they're doing. They're trying to change things, and it's time we put a stop to it!"

John paused to take in the reaction of his audience. They were angry. He knew that. If they weren't, they wouldn't have come. They were scared, too. The sound of the chain brought home just how serious and hopeless their situation was.

John pointed to the chain. "I don't want this anymore than you do, but they've left us no choice! They as much as put this chain around *our* necks, so we have no choice but to do the same to them." John stepped aside to introduce the old man who'd gaveled this meeting to order. "You all have probably seen Aaron around town. I don't know if you've ever talked to him, but he has some experience in these things." He yielded the floor. "Aaron."

The old man always had a distant look in his eye, like something was on his mind. Usually, that made him appear a little crazy. Tonight he looked wise. His wrinkled eyes held experiences that he longed to share with these sympathetic men. "I grew up in Mississippi. I was ten years old in 1963 when the bombings hit Alabama. By that time, we in Mississippi had been waist deep in the shit. I seen some things."

The men in the room silently contemplated what this old man had seen as a young one.

"There's an art to a lynching," said old man Aaron. "I should know. I seen a few." His memories lightened his mood, as evidenced by the new spark in his voice. "So what you boys aimin' to do?"

"How you mean, Aaron?" asked John.

"I mean, are you looking to get information, or are you trying to send a message?" Aaron hadn't lived in Mississippi since the 1980s, but his southern accent clung to his voice like moss on a swamp Cypress.

"Send a message," shouted Ned, a high school junior some locals believed was destined to follow in John's footsteps. "We don't want no information from them."

"Is the sheriff on our side, or do we have to do this quick-like?" asked Aaron.

John answered. "He ain't come right out and said it, but he as much as told me his phone won't hold a charge tonight."

"Good." Aaron smiled. "We can take our time." He took a length of chain and stretched it, as if testing its quality. "When I was a kid, I witnessed three lynchings. My Daddy said I'd seen about every variety."

His audience hung on his every word. Before the current troubles, not one of them would have given Aaron a second look. Now he was a hero of the Southern fight against the Civil Rights movement. In this new war, these young minds were eager to learn the old ways.

"You got your boy facing the tree, facing out from the tree, or just a regular hangin' and beatin'." He took Ned by the shoulders, spun him around to face John, and pushed them together. "John, you're the tree."

"Good casting," said an anonymous observer, and the men all laughed.

Aaron put Ned's hands behind his back, gently wrapped them with the chains and gave it a little tug. "You see here. If you're in a hurry, you just hook this chain up to the back of the car and drive away. If it don't pull his arms off completely, it'll back-snap his sternum, and the chain—you wrap the chain around him and the tree—it'll dig two or three inches into him. Break his spine, crush his innards. It don't matter if they find him right away, he'll be dead by morning."

"That's what I'm talking about!" said another anonymous man.

Aaron wasn't done with the lesson. "The way I saw it done was slow. They just pulled on them chains a little bit, and pretty soon, POP!" Everyone jumped. Aaron laughed. "One shoulder snapped out of joint, and that boy screamed bloody murder—which reminds me, know your neighborhood. You don't want one of their kind as a witness."

"Why not?" asked one of Ned's classmates. "It's not like they're going to swear on no Bible." Everyone laughed.

John stayed closer to serious. "We'll gag 'em just the same."

"Good," said the classmate. From the grin on his face it was clear he'd been encouraged by his response. "I don't want to hear that gibberish comin' out of their mouths anyway."

"The other way to do it," said Aaron, "is with his back to the tree." He turned Ned around to face him, and gave him a shove into John. "If you're in a hurry, you wrap the chain around his neck and pull from the backside. Again, you can hook it up to the car. That'll cut his head clean off."

"Hot damn!"

"Or… you can wrap the chain around his body and pull until it touches wood, if you know what I mean." Another laugh.

"Or, you can just hang him and beat the shit out of him. By the way, when he dies, that's what's going to happen, the shit's going to come all out of him, so stand clear."

"They've been spewing shit all their lives, why should their deaths be any different?" That got the kid a cheer.

Aaron gave John a subtle nod. Time for him to take over.

"That's right," said John. "This is a Christian Nation, am I right?"

"Right!"

"They want to change that!"

"Hell no!"

"We speak English around here," said John.

"That's right!"

"We have a right to bear arms, and tonight we're going to use them!"

"That's right."

John had them in a frenzy. It was time to drive it home. "From now on, no scientist is safe! We'll kill them and their theories!"

"Kill 'em!"

"Find me a college professor with his million dollar education, and we'll nail him to a tree!"

"Kill 'em!"

"Kill the lawyers!"

"Kill 'em!"

"They tell lies about global warming. We're going to teach them the truth about how hot it is in Satan's house!"

"That's right!"

"They say we're out of oil, that we have to drive them electric cars made in Japan. But I tell you what, we've got enough oil to light their fancy clothes on fire."

"With them in 'em!"

"That's right!"

"Now let's do God's work and send all those pansy-assed intellectuals to hell!"

"Kill 'em!"

There's something unique about the sound of a chain. Each link, individually so delicate, makes a harmless, charming ting. But when slammed together, they speak with a different voice.

A SECRET KEPT IN SHAME

A.M. Supinger

CHÊTULAN SUCKED IN THE SWEET smoke of deadweed, knowing the three men in front of him were terrified of its fumes; he blew a stream of it into their faces just to watch them scramble from its path. The eerie white smoke looked like a vengeful ghost until it dissipated, leaving only the cloying scent of death in its wake.

Unlike the quivering cowards who called themselves chieftains, Chêtulan had nothing to fear. His mortality hinged on less tangible dangers. Still, he stopped puffing on the pipe. He was looking at three *men* instead of the three *maidens* he'd been promised. "Where are my brides?"

"The girls and their trousseaus are on the way—they'll be here at dawn." Gregor was the bravest of the leaders, a man used to commanding absolute respect. Of all the free lands, his had been the hardest to conquer. "Before they get here, we wanted to make sure the agreement is intact."

Chêtulan chuckled. The ten skulls making up his mask distorted the sound—to the chieftains, his voice was closer to that of a demon than a man. "I see your reasons for what they are, Gregor. You wanted to test your theory."

The hulking chieftain didn't bother to deny it. He met Chêtulan's stare with unflinching hatred. "Aye."

Chêtulan chuckled, not bothering to protest the wait again.

Daybreak slowly banished shadows back to the afterworld, but Sŭnt did the chieftains no favors; as their god ascended into the sky, his divine glory mocked the men's pallor. The moon itself could not have compared to their bloodless faces—as if *they* were the sacrifices.

"As you can see, Death does not bow to Sŭnt."

Gregor shuddered at the colorful honorific. As the Unborn King, Chêtulan had been named *foul* and *unholy* by those who feared him—but Death had become his most feared title. Terror caked the tongues of those who spoke his names.

The gates of Gregor's city opened, and three carts rolled out. The horses were each led by a girl—his brides.

"May Sŭnt have mercy on them," Gregor murmured. "And us."

"Don't be greedy," Chêtulan mocked. "Already you're at *my* mercy."

As the wagons drew closer, the piles of gold behind the girls became evident. Chêtulan grinned. He adored treasure more than any dragon. One of his armies was devoted solely to guarding his trove. A hum of anticipation rumbled in his chest; the soldiers at his back shifted along with his mood. They were restless and ready to return home.

Chêtulan grinned at the thought of taking all three wagons home. It would be a true pleasure to dump this tithe atop all the others he'd amassed. But the girls…they would be a nuisance. Chêtulan turned from watching his gold and whistled for his mother. She hurried forward, her frame wobbling in her excitement.

She'd asked for this boon years ago, before he'd risen to claim the title of Unborn King. As a warring youth, brides had no appeal to him. But Chêtulan had promised to wed once his throne was secure… and he'd honor that, no matter how unappealing the task.

"You're responsible for them," he told her. "Inspect each for flaws—I'll not accept anything less than perfection." Even if the creatures were flesh blobs. He heaved a sigh at the thought of being around the women and then tucked away his annoyance. An oath was an oath.

The chieftains stared in horror at Chêtulan's mother, their faces slack and pupils blown. As if they'd never seen a ghoul before. Chêtulan rolled his eyes. He knew firsthand how many of the undead had raided their cities—certainly more than enough for the men to have grown accustomed to pearly bones.

"Why is it wearing a *dress*?" Gregor whispered. Transfixed, he watched the crimson silk caress Chêtulan's mother.

The wagons' arrival broke the moment, and the chieftains ushered the girls forward. By how swiftly they moved, each man seemed at the end of his rope. Yet, Chêtulan didn't miss the way Gregor's hand lingered, or the way his eyes softened. The sacrifice from Gregor's city was important to the man, a *personal* tithe.

Taking her was suddenly satisfying.

"Before we give them to you, ease our minds—tell us you'll keep your end of the agreement." Gregor still hadn't let go of the girl, who was silently staring at the ground, even though the other two chieftains were already backing away.

"You asked for mercy, not a wet nurse. Stop sniveling." Chêtulan gestured for his mother to examine the girls.

Compared to the men, all three maidens were tiny. It had been a long time since Chêtulan had seen a living woman, so it surprised him how petite they were. It also struck him as odd that such delicate creatures were responsible for bringing life into the world.

The girls were all dressed in simple black gowns—mourning clothes; the irony was not lost on him—and their hair was unbound. At first glance, all three were alike…too alike. Their flesh bore the darker hue of mountain folk, and their bodies were similar in shape and height. Chêtulan was bored before seeing their faces, sure that none of them could stir his passion.

But his mother ignored his indifference and went to circle the girls. Though her skeleton was bare of muscle, fat, and skin, she moved like a lithe dancer; the sound of her joints grinding together was the only distraction from her graceful stride.

"What is it doing?" Gregor demanded. He stepped forward, as if to ward off the ghoul, but couldn't seem to make himself actually touch the bare bones.

"Be silent," Chêtulan commanded. The other two chieftains weren't half as bothersome. They looked uncomfortable, but didn't dare question him.

His mother never touched the maidens as she inspected their potential. While alive, she'd been a *hetia* wise in the ways of magic. Her soul had kept the ability even after death, and Chêtulan trusted her to guide his choices. Theirs was a bond not dependent on a pulse.

Her bones rattled as she stepped to his side. A slow hiss whistled through her teeth, and Chêtulan cocked his head as she reported her findings. One girl had a black aura, meaning fate would soon claim her for the grave. Another of the sacrifices had aura more bloody than his own, which he didn't know how to interpret. The last girl was green and gold, shining with innocence and hope that his mother found enchanting.

He didn't want a dead bride—he had enough corpses to keep him company. He whistled for his mother to usher the fated one away from the other two. The chit looked up in confusion, as if asking why. "You're fated to die young. Go home and enjoy what time you have left," Chêtulan said to her.

Tears rolled down her cheeks even as relief radiated from her. He waved his hand, dismissing her, and one of the quiet chieftains strode forward to claim the girl. He hurried back toward the village with her, as if Chêtulan might change his mind.

Mimicking his mother's earlier path around the remaining maidens, Chêtulan found little to admire. Unlike those born to the living, he had no natural magic. Though he might have been a great *hetia* in different circumstances, he had nothing but his eyes to judge the world. Bones spoke to him in ways flesh could not—he found the softness of the living to be strange and ugly.

His brides were no exception.

Chêtulan couldn't even tell them apart, except that Gregor was watching his little sacrifice with sorrow. It made Chêtulan curious. His bone-white fingers chucked the girl's chin gently, and she lifted her face for the first time.

Chêtulan almost stumbled back in surprise.

She was fleshy and small, her bones wrapped in an unappealing tan package, but her face…he'd never seen anything like it. Narrowed, angry eyes stared up at him, but Chêtulan ignored the challenge in those green depths. Her ebony lashes were long and thick, and they fluttered like the wings of a frantic butterfly as the girl fought to contain her rage. Her lips were red—not stained or painted, but naturally red. The color of blood. That alone would have been enticing, but her features were set within a bone structure to rival no other. Her chin was dainty before flaring out to a softly curved jaw, but her cheekbones were high and sharp. The contrast should have been too jarring, but it highlighted the gentle slope of her nose. The graceful arch of her eyebrows.

She was the most unusual, striking beauty he'd ever seen. And she was *his*.

Chêtulan grinned behind his mask, glad the girl couldn't see his expression. No doubt he looked as feral as he suddenly felt. His bride was captivating. The other chit could only fall short. "I'll take this one. She'll buy all three villages one month of peace. After that, you must begin tithing."

"No!" Gregor protested. "You said we'd have until solstice!"

The army at Chêtulan's back creaked and groaned as the mass of bones prepared to leap forward and fight. All it would take was a word. "Before offering a sacrifice, use a *hetia* to guide your decision. It is a lesson you should learn well, for I will not excuse the same mistake twice."

"You want more maidens?" Gregor's alarm made his voice loud, and several of the ghouls made strange, hair-raising noises in response. Without tongues, their battle cries were like Death's trumpets, and it sent pleasant chills down Chêtulan's spine. Gregor, however, flinched.

"If I do, you will offer them." There was no doubt that the chieftains would obey. "Say your goodbyes."

He turned from the living so he would not have to watch their sorrow. He had no interest in tears. The bony skulls of his army stretched out like ashy foam atop a dead sea. It was beautiful. Powerful. Not for the first time, Chêtulan was glad to be The Unborn King.

He whistled for his ghouls to tend the wagons and ensure his gold made it home. They jumped to obey, and Gregor's shout of surprise made Chêtulan grin. Then he felt the warmth of his bride at his back. She didn't speak or touch him, but her presence somehow soothed his spirit.

Mother had been right: having a bride was a good thing.

Chêtulan drew his warped magic from deep within. It was curdled, as always. The *hetia* magic that should have been his had died alongside his mother during childbirth, attached to her soul as it passed from the living world. Because his natural magic never took up residence, Death had seeped into its place.

After clawing his way free of his mother's corpse, Chêtulan had accepted his lot in life. Even as an infant, he'd straddled the edge between the living and dead. As an Unborn, he was burdened from his first breath with dark magic and all its knowledge...which is how he'd locked his mother's soul to her dead body. Her ghoul had been the first of many that he'd collected into armies.

Now legions of ghouls fulfilled his every whim.

He relished that power, even as hail pelted down from the storm his magic conjured. The thick chunks of ice bounced harmlessly off his bone mask and the bodies of his undead army, but he heard his bride grunt when struck. Without thinking, he drew her beneath his arm. She shuddered but didn't protest the protection, even when the air violently crackled with power. A bolt of lightning hit the ground in front of them, hissing and writhing instead of discharging.

In all the world, there was nothing more beautiful than a soul. Chêtulan had seen countless people die, and still he was struck by their essence upon death. And that's what made up the bolts of angry energy: souls of the damned. They were frighteningly lovely, and he took a moment to admire their rage. Inside the white light, the souls were pulsating with their need for vengeance—or whatever it was that drove the damned to eternal suffering.

He didn't pity them. Only fools pitied the dead.

"We're going to walk through," he murmured to his bride. "Close your eyes and hold onto me." Without waiting for an answer, he strode forward with her still tucked under his arm. She flinched when the lightning buzzed across their skin, but his little beauty was brave. No sobs, praise the dead.

Once through the portal, he kept moving forward; the ghouls poured through after them, ambling home like lazy dogs in need of a good place to nap. Even his mother wandered off. "You can open your eyes," he told the petite creature in his arms.

Her gasp was supremely satisfying.

Though she—and the other two girls—were called sacrifices by their people, it had always been his plan to indulge his brides. After years of war, his spoils were piled high enough to rival the tallest mountain. Life would be easy for his beautiful *sacrifice*.

She stepped away from him to look around. His castle was tucked deep within the Demon Mountains, named for the gloomy grey mist that never lifted—and for his ghouls. But Lightning Peak was anything but grey. Sculptures erupted from the mountain, created by innumerable portals; the ice and lightening solidified with the help of magic, creating macabre masterpieces. The morning sun set fire to the jagged monuments of the damned and cast wicked light like a prism.

Chêtulan studied the girl as she took it all in. "Do you like it?" he asked. His bride didn't answer, but her silence didn't bother him. He doubted she'd ever seen anything like his home, just as he'd never seen anyone like her. "What's your name?" He was curious to see if it matched her beauty.

She glared over his shoulder, anger still brightening her green eyes. "Whatever you wish it be."

Her beauty was intriguing and unique, but the girl needed to learn respect. "Perhaps your screams as I beat you will suffice as a name."

"Do your worst," she spat. No fear crept into her gaze, and he admired her bravery again, even as it infuriated him.

"No wonder Gregor was willing to give you away." The man's sorrowful gaze had been an act, and Chêtulan had been duped by it.

She snorted—her delicate little nose wrinkling as she made the sound. "You stole years of training from him. He bought me when I was ten, and has *tutored* me ever since."

His mother would have sensed if the girl was other than chaste, so his bride had to be lying. Slaves were naught but playthings. But why would she claim that status if it were not true? It made no sense. Chêtulan studied her tense shoulders and clenched jaw. She all but hummed with aggression. "What name did Gregor use?"

She didn't answer immediately, but something about the way she held herself—as if on a precipice—kept Chêtulan from shaking it out of her. And then she shuddered, as if weary of some inner battle. "Atoya."

A secret kept in shame.

As Unborn, he understood shame…and suddenly understood her anger. He doubted her "tutoring" had left anything but a thin barrier of innocence; her virgin's blood would have fetched a fortune. No wonder her bloody aura matched his own. His mother's *hetia* once again proved its worth.

A touch of wistfulness softened her posture when she looked back at his castle. "I'd thought you'd kill me; that's what Gregor said you'd do. Cut my soul from my body while I was alive so you could bind it to you for eternity." Chêtulan rolled his eyes. "I never considered I'd be alive this long…having a conversation about *names*, of all things."

He moved behind her, drawn by her anguish, and set his hands upon her shoulders. "I was seeking companionship, not souls, when I bargained for brides." He pulled her back against his chest and then wrapped his arms around her slender frame. "Of all the women in the world, fate brought you to me."

"Fate brought you three women," she whispered, her anger tempered by curiosity. "And you chose me…" Her words trailed off, but he knew what she was asking.

"My mother—the ghoul in the red dress—said you have an aura much like my own. Even if nothing but that links us, it's more than many other couples share." He turned her so that she was looking up at him. "Pick a name without shame attached to it. From this moment on, that is who you'll be."

She stared at him, trying to see the man behind his mask. "What is your name?" she asked.

"Death, Unborn King, Monster, Revenant, and Beast were all given to me by strangers. Chêtulan is what my mother would have called me." It was a private name, one that no other living person knew.

"It is a strong name; she chose well," his bride said. And then she shrugged, as if unsure how to put her thoughts into words. "I was sold to Gregor without a name…it never bothered me to be called his shameful secret. The truth felt kinder than being gifted with a sweet name. The only other moniker that would have suited me was Bitterness." Her lips twisted into a smile. "But there was a girl…poor and uglier than a warty dog, her entire life was one miserable struggle after another to make ends meet. I admired her strength. Even though she had less than me—a slave—she was kind. I don't know how she found the will, but she never went a day without laughing."

Fury ignited in her eyes, stoked as if a blacksmith had tried to melt down emeralds. Chêtulan ran his thumb along her jaw. "What happened to her?"

"She was in the wrong place at the wrong time. Her face, which hid so much kindness, disgusted Gregor when he stumbled upon her." Chêtulan's bride shook her head as if to clear away bad memories. "I've always remembered her, though, even when others forgot. Probably because Ugly Everlet was never ashamed."

For some reason, her story touched him even as it angered him. He cupped her face between his palms. "Ask it of me, and I will bring you Gregor's head."

She pulled away. "I would never forgive you."

His bride was a confusing creature. Chêtulan tamped down the swell of emotions she'd evoked and strode past her, toward his castle. He didn't have time for her games. "We'll find you a room and—"

"His head belongs to me," she murmured. "I would rip it off with my own two hands if I could."

Chêtulan paused; he could understand that. Admire it, even. "Your bloodthirsty nature appeals to me, Bride." He held out his hand to her, a peace offering.

"Everlet," she said, and then took his hand.

He stroked his thumb across her palm. "My bloodthirsty Everlet." He was so taken with her in that moment, so enamored, that he wanted to give her vengeance. "If you truly want his death, we shall go back for it."

"Now?" The angry willfulness from moments before was replaced with childlike eagerness. Chêtulan laughed aloud at the hope brightening her face. She smiled, showing two dimples he hadn't known she possessed.

Shaking his head at how quickly he'd fallen under her spell, Chêtulan drew on his dark magic. A single whistle drew twenty of his ghouls, and they crowded close as the hail began to plummet. Everlet ducked beneath his shoulder without persuading, her little body easily protected by his girth.

When the lightning hit, she all but leapt forward. Chêtulan chuckled as they went through once more, the familiar sizzle of the damned souls as comforting as a mother's embrace. His ghouls encircled them once the portal closed, guarding against the empty field that stretched in front of Gregor's walls.

"We'll have to wait for a while," he warned Everlet. The chieftain liked to keep Chêtulan waiting as long as possible; it was the only power the foolish man possessed.

"I doubt it—not once he sees me. He spent a fortune on my education." Her tone was sour, as if speaking of him left a bad taste in her mouth. "If there's any chance of reclaiming me, he'll take it."

As Everlet predicted, the gates opened mere moments later. Gregor rode out alongside the other two chieftains, and the three of them looked terrified. Yet, Gregor couldn't keep his eyes from Everlet. He went so far as to lick his lips, and Chêtulan felt gratified in knowing she would kill him for it.

"What brings you back?" Gregor asked, his eyes never leaving Chêtulan's bride.

Everlet smiled, her beautiful face lit with joy. If not for the feral glint in her eyes, Chêtulan would have said she looked angelic. "Revenge," she purred.

Gregor paled and tried to wheel his horse around, but Chêtulan whistled for his ghouls to drag him from the beast. Without looking away from the fool on the ground, Chêtulan told the other two chieftains to leave. They fled, Gregor's horse trailing after them.

"Let go! Please!" the fool screamed. "Let me go!"

The ghouls hissed out their laughter and held firm. Gregor's pleas were like music to them.

Everlet, who had stayed tucked beneath Chêtulan's arm, stepped forward. She stared down at the chieftain in silence. She could have been carved from fury itself, like a beautiful monument to wrath.

She was still for so long that Chêtulan wondered if she'd lost her nerve. "Do you want me to do it?" he asked.

Her glare was answer enough. "He forced me to learn every degrading act a woman can know," she whispered. "And he killed *her*." With tears in her eyes, Everlet turned fully to Chêtulan. "One moment of pain isn't enough—I want him to suffer."

Chêtulan cupped her cheek with one hand. "Ask it of me, and it's yours."

She pulled one of the many daggers from Chêtulan's belt, her tiny hand gripping it fiercely. His bride was no trembling lamb; Everlet was like a tigress who'd discovered her claws. Gregor didn't appear to appreciate her savage beauty in that moment—he thrashed against the ghouls in an attempt to flee her vengeance.

"Your soul will wither long before it goes free," she vowed as she knelt next to Gregor's pale face. "And it's still better than you deserve." Slowly—as if relishing the blood—she drew the blade across his throat. The chieftain gurgled as his windpipe flooded, but death claimed him quickly. All too soon he was still and silent.

Chêtulan watched Gregor's soul writhe within his corpse. Like a snake shedding skin, the iridescent spirit wormed its way out of the dead flesh. But once free, it couldn't go anywhere. Like all souls, Gregor was attached to his body until the next solstice. Or until an Unborn swept him up.

It was as easy as breathing to call upon his curdled magic; like thousands of times before, Chêtulan plucked a thin cord of the putrid power, much like yanking a hair from his head. He used it to tether Gregor's soul to his dead body, despite how the newly dead man tried to struggle.

Gregor's body lurched, his face slack as his soul sought to tear free of its undead host.

"And a ghoul is born," Chêtulan chuckled. He turned to see his bride's reaction, and almost fell back when she launched herself into his arms. Chêtulan grinned as Everlet scrambled to wrap herself around him in an enthusiastic hug. "Let's go home," he whispered into her hair.

She pulled back and pouted, her face splattered with

blood. She'd never been more adorable. "Let's go make more!" she countered. "I know some other people who have it coming!"

"You're a bloodthirsty little thing." Not that he minded. "But even Death needs rest."

Her cheeky smile was dangerous—a weapon all its own. "Maybe tomorrow?"

"You have only to ask." With gentle fingers, he smeared the blood across her cheek; it matched her red lips perfectly. When her tiny, pink tongue flicked out to lick a drop away, Chêtulan groaned.

She bit her lip, seeming shy for the first time. "...will you take me home?"

THE GODS WITHIN
Justin Holley

"**Y**OU CAN'T GO SEE 'EM, Mathis," Roger said, his head shaking back and forth. He shrugged and rolled his eyes.

Mathis tried his best to look like he didn't give a shit about the Union rules when, in fact, he cared a great deal. To Mathis, Roger was like a spider—a round head surrounded by oversize appendages. Frustrated, Mathis ran his fingers over the dark stubble on his chin. It'd be a miracle if he didn't lose his temper. "Why not?" he asked. "They work for Petersheim Manufacturing, don't they?"

"They work for the Union," Roger reminded him. He grinned, the smile nothing but a slight widening of his tiny mouth, like the action hurt him. "Besides, what's the problem? You got bad product or what?"

"No," Mathis said, reluctantly, "but goddamn it, Roger, nobody's even met with the maintenance team in—in, who knows how long. I can't even send a team inside the facility to inspect."

"And why would you? If you allow people inside, then you gotta open yourself up to federal safety inspections." Roger raised an eyebrow, steepled his fingers.

"The maintenance team sure as hell goes inside there!"

"Yes," Roger agreed, "but they work for us. The Union!"

Mathis ran a hand through his short dark hair. "Doesn't HR at least have the right to visit, now and again, with the crew that keeps our equipment functional? It is our equipment."

"That's what you pay *us* for, Mathis," Roger said quietly. "So, unless your customers are complaining, I suggest you just relax." He took a deep breath and smiled. "Look, I know you gotta rattle my cage now and again, gotta justify your existence. But don't worry about it. The facility was sealed for good reason. Keep it that way, okay?"

Mathis nodded.

Roger smiled even bigger, clapped Mathis on the back like he were nothing but a pouting child, then turned and walked toward the door. Just short of the exit, Roger turned. "See ya next month?" he asked. "Maybe we can visit over a mug of IPA—or a round of cyber-golf."

Mathis hated to be placated. He crumpled a sheet of paper and barely kept from throwing it at Roger's bulbous head. "Maybe you can explain to me what your employees look like, at least."

"Or maybe not," Roger called as he swung through the door.

Mathis nodded, then waved him out. Once Roger disappeared, Mathis let out the breath he'd been holding. He thought about the situation, not sure whether he liked it or not. Seventeen years ago the Union had sealed the facility, leaving nothing inside but the technological advances promised by the supplier who built the machines, fully automated: no more need for employees. Except, of course, those needed to maintain the automation. And the Union had happily obliged to supply them. Some decision made in a burst of blind madness, no doubt brought on by some perceived financial windfall.

The ownership group could go hang, Mathis thought.

Sure, Petersheim still employed the workers who received raw materials and shipped out product, but none of them ever set foot inside production. In fact, there were no doors, only large elevators the receiving crew used to shuttle in raw materials, and the big conveyors on which the finished product trundled out. Somehow, the machines inside did everything else.

Mathis's phone rang; he rolled his eyes.

"Mathis!" he said, more irritable than he cared for.

"Yeah, hey," the man on the other end said, voice heavy and full of gravel. "We found some more."

"Some more what?" he asked. But he knew. Mathis picked up his stapler, running a thumb over the black cool steel, felt the wave of cold race through his gut like ice-water.

The man, Tom Sand from shipping, didn't answer. Mathis could hear him breathing heavily on the other end, like saying the words might conjure up something.

"Never mind," Mathis said. "I'll be right out."

Tom Sand hung up.

Mathis looked at the receiver in his hand, thought of smashing it against the wall, then cradled it and stood up. This was exactly the thing he'd wanted to argue about with Roger. Now he wished he hadn't changed his mind—wished he hadn't let himself be cowed. No, the product wasn't out of specification, but it sure as hell wasn't right.

Mathis stood up, his knees clearing the edge of his old-fashioned oak desk by the slimmest of margins. His office chair spun off behind him as if trying to escape Mathis's foul mood. Determined, he strode out his office door and made for the reception desk. As he walked, Mathis wondered why the ownership group hadn't also decided to automate reception if it was so damn prudent and cost-effective to do so. Reaching the desk, he stared at the redhead behind it.

"I don't think I care for the look in your eye, Mathis," she said with a tight smile. "Roger piss you off again?"

Mathis ran a hand through his hair, let out a breath.

"Look what he gave me," she said, excited. She held out a bouquet of orange and yellow Asiatic lilies. "He might be a douche, but he's a douche with good taste, no?"

"Oh, a real charmer all right," Mathis said. He imagined spider legs sprouting from the man's temples, then quickly decided not to verbalize such a horrid image. Might as well allow Carly her untarnished image. "Hold my calls. I'm going out to shipping."

"Oh?" she asked, staring at Mathis like he'd suddenly grown horns. That got her attention. "Something to do with Roger?"

"Something to do with the Union," Mathis quipped. "So by extension, yes."

"Is it more of—you know?" Carly started, not able to say the word. Mathis noticed her flinch and her green eyes narrow.

He nodded with a subtle bob of his head, cryptic. "I'll be back for my eleven-hundred interview."

"Where's it all coming from, do you think?"

"Why do you think I'm going over to shipping?" he asked, turning for the air-locked doors. "I'll be back."

"Sure," he heard her say, and then Mathis was into the vestibule, the sliding glass of the interior door closing with a hiss behind him. He moved toward the thick exterior door, complete with sun-shielding to prevent damage to the vestibule carpeting. Everyone knew by now, the sun wasn't any kinder to the more gentle fabrics than it was to the skin. Mathis, thankful for his PF100 lotion, slapped his palm on the exit grid. The light above the door went from red to yellow to green before the door finally slid open with a hurricane blast of vacuumed air.

The heat felt blistering as it washed over Mathis, and the blood-red sun had barely risen above the scant trees that surrounded the man-made pond in the yard.

The sun appeared bloated, its red bottom so deep Mathis imagined slicing it open toward the bottom and allowing the blood-red juice to rain down onto the parched Earth.

Mathis sighed. The scientists blamed it on the depleted atmosphere, the lack of ozone, but everyone knew the sun would fail—someday. But probably not today. So Mathis hopped into the old golf cart, a remnant from the old days when golf was still played in the great outdoors. He knew he ought to take the air-conditioned tram to the production plant, but Mathis loved the feel of being in complete control, the wheel in his hand, the hot breeze in his hair, the dust blowing behind him like a vapor trail. Never mind the severe wind and sun burns he'd receive for his troubles. *Infernal!*

Despite the mind-numbing heat of midday, Mathis negotiated the cracked and sand-weathered ribbon of asphalt, picking his way around the south end of the admin building. The ownership group had long ago decided not to maintain any of the old transportation infrastructure, but the tarmac remained usable—a minor miracle in Mathis's opinion.

The shipping end of Petersheim's production facility came into view first, then, as Mathis edged around the corner, the rest of the pre-cast concrete monolith slithered into his sightline. Not a single sign of human habitation showed itself, all operations long ago confined indoors. Mathis thought the place looked haunted and ghastly. But he had to admit the Union maintenance employees did an adequate job of upkeep, even on the exterior. Somehow, though, the building still looked wrong. Like a rich child left to be raised by the nanny, he thought.

With a burst of speed, induced for the most part by Mathis's desire to show off his minor rebellion to the shipping crew, he motored toward one of the huge bay doors where the industrial trams launched. Mathis didn't care for their tube-like blue and silver bodies because they were an affront to the old ways of semi-trucks and railways. Call him a dinosaur, but he could still get things done.

Before disappearing inside, Mathis looked down the length of the concrete building and wondered absently where shipping ended and production began. He was pretty sure it correlated directly with the area where any type of windows or openings ceased. Machines didn't need light—especially natural light. No vitamin D needed, Mathis thought wildly. And then he motored up the steep concrete ramp to one of the bay doors.

The big door opened just enough to allow him entrance. He knew the vacuum and air systems would work overtime to account for the hot air, but Mathis couldn't have cared less. He enjoyed being a pain in the ass. Through the Plexiglas ceiling of his golf cart, Mathis watched as he drove under the massive door. For an instant he could see the exterior and interior all at once. The sight was glorious, like looking up the side of a giant cliff-face.

Inside, Tom Sand stood on the loading floor, large fists on his bony hips, a scowl cut deep in his face like he'd been born with it. His large work boots scuffed impatiently at the concrete floor.

Mathis brought the golf cart to an abrupt halt, the back tires leaving a skid mark behind. The action made him feel like a teenager with his first car. Behind him the giant bay door descended, hydraulics grinding away from somewhere above.

"The hell you drive that thing over here for?" Tom said. His voice sounded just as gravely as on the phone, maybe more so. "You're letting all the infernal air in."

"Fresh air is good for you," Mathis said. "Didn't your mama teach ya that?"

"Not that air. Government boys say more 'n three weeks cumulative a year'll kill you. Something or another about toxins and skin cancer..."

"We all gotta go sometime." Mathis wiped sweat from his face. "And if God wanted me inside all the goddamn time he'd a made me a house cat. Anyway, show me."

"God ain't got anything to do with this." Tom turned on his right foot and walked to a long cart filled with steel door sections.

Mathis looked at the forty-foot slabs, small by industrial standards nowadays. In the old days, every house had a residential garage door. They were staples. Now Petersheim Inc. had to cater to big industry, supply them with the big, thick—and ugly in his opinion—airtight thermal bay-doors. They still went up and down, but utilized hydraulics. Garage doors were a thing of the past—like him and Tom. It wasn't lost on him that perhaps they'd been at all this for too long. Then he noticed the brown streaks.

"See, here's what I'm talkin' about, Mathis." Tom pointed at the discoloration. "I thought nobody worked up in there." He pointed to the thirty-foot ceiling where the sections came out of production through a gate just big enough for them to fit through, then rode the massive black-rubber conveyers down to ground level.

"Whadya figure it is?"

Tom shrugged. "Gotta be blood—dried."

Mathis shrugged and muttered, "Could be." He glanced upward as a section breeched the gate.

"That ain't all," Tom added, then stared at Mathis.

"What?"

"We've been hearing things."

"Things?"

"Things we ought not hear from in there," Tom said. "Things like voices. Yesterday Brandt heard a baby crying, came got me, and sure as hell there it was, plain as day."

"Could've been the maintenance team, I suppose," Mathis reasoned. "They must go in there to do their preventative maintenance and such."

"And they just scream—and cry like a newborn for the hell of it?" Tom folded his arms over his chest. "Maybe they had the family in for a picnic. C'mon, don't you think we'd know the sounds of routine maintenance when we hear it? Most of us have been here long as you have." He paused, ran a hand over his stubbly chin. "Maybe we oughta call the cops."

"The cops?" Mathis asked. "Oh, come on, Tom. I'll go up and see the maintenance supervisor before I do that. It's our facility."

"That what you told that schlep Roger Goodwin?" he asked, staring Mathis in the eye.

Mathis looked away.

"Or maybe we oughta just wipe 'em down again, get 'em on the road," Tom said, ignoring Mathis's non-reply. "Heaven knows Aker Door's installation boys'll have our balls if we're late like last time."

"It's not like we're talking about a spot of grease, or a smudge of glue here," Mathis said. "Blood, babies crying, men screaming. Something's going on in there, and I think Roger knows what it is." He glanced back up at the thin slit of darkness leading to production. When product wasn't coming through, a set of bars dropped into place like teeth in a grin. "Aker's installers will have to wait. And no, you damn well know I didn't tell Roger."

"Why? You scared of him?"

"No," Mathis lied. "He's just…unnerving. And every time I intend to let him have it, well, he goads me and I lose focus. But screw Roger!"

"What do you have in mind, then?" Tom asked.

Mathis nodded and ran a trembling hand through his short brown hair. Now that was a damn good question. He knew pissing off the Union could get him in some real hot-water with the ownership group, not to mention the government. But so could blood smeared on the product. No way to clean it all off, and last time Aker Door had called and complained to him personally, wanted to know who got butchered making their products. Mathis had joked about it, reassured them. And they'd seemed okay, but, Mathis knew, next time they'd call the owners.

He couldn't win. So, since he would be in trouble either way, then, by God, he'd go down swinging. Plus, didn't he have an ethical responsibility to find the root cause of all the blood and screams? And if the maintenance team wouldn't let him investigate, then he would call the cops, and see how they liked them apples.

Finally, Mathis said, "I'm going in there." He glanced up at the gate at the top of the industrial conveyor.

"Not through there, you're not."

"No," Mathis said firmly. "I'm going right to the maintenance office and demand answers."

Tom stared Mathis in the eye, and nodded his head. "Let's go."

The tram dropped them off on a concrete platform off the west side of the long building, equidistant between the shipping and receiving ends. Mathis glanced nervously at the elevator doors, which seemed the only way to reach the maintenance office thirty feet above. There were no buttons to push, no way to call the elevator car. Only a lonely call box with a fairly ancient handset, both covered in dust and grime.

Mathis wondered if it even worked anymore.

"You gonna ring 'em?" Tom asked, pointing at the handset.

Mathis let out a breath, then nodded. He grabbed the handset and then removed the filthy thing from its cradle with a dull click.

"Hurry the hell up," Tom said. "It's hotter than the hubs of hell out here, and I only wore my SPF seventy-five lotion today."

The cup Mathis placed on his already reddening ear felt like a hot-iron on his skin. Great, now he'd get a blister for sure. His wife would be so pleased. No, he thought, Maggie would understand. She was a good woman. Suddenly, going up into the bowels of the production facility—where blood oozed and screams echoed—no longer sounded like such a great idea. Mathis swallowed his growing fear and listened to the phone ring once, twice, all the way to ten. Just when he thought nobody would answer, someone actually did.

"Yeah," a dull, scratchy voice said.

"Um, yeah," Mathis said. "This here is the GM for Petersheim. I need a word with your supervisor, I'm afraid." Mathis thought he'd sounded authoritative and not as nervous as he felt.

A loud click burst through the ear-piece, and then a steady dial tone.

The douche hung up on me, Mathis thought. But then the elevator door slid open without a sound, the inside immaculate and well-kept, not a spot on the waxed white linoleum. Mathis stared down and caught his own reflection, the look of awe in his own eyes. The scent of lilac and cherry blossoms came to his nose and brought him back to his childhood, to his grandmother's yard. That was before the world had cannibalized its own ozone layer. Industry had done the world few favors. He looked back at Tom, who appeared about as shocked as Mathis felt.

"You coming?" Mathis asked.

"Depends," Tom answered. "What's the catch?"

Mathis shrugged. "I'm going up, so come or not."

With a huff, Tom stepped beside him and they entered the car together. The door slid shut immediately, nearly clipped their asses, and he heard Tom make a little squeaky noise, which seemed out of character for the usually tough SOB.

Mathis got goose bumps. Not because it was cold in the elevator, but because if something could scare ol' Tom, then maybe that something oughtn't be trifled with. But they were already on the way up, and Mathis could see no way to reverse the situation, not a single lit button. So he set his jaw and stared at his reflection in the stainless steel wall, trying to strike some pose that didn't make him look like a scared little kid. The floor vibrated only slightly beneath their feet, until finally, the car came to a gradual stop.

That's when the door opened.

Mathis felt himself react, a cold terror filling his belly like ice-water. He tried to recover, smoothing out his khakis, taking a deep breath. It didn't matter because nobody was there to greet them, only a shadowy, dimly lit foyer. Mathis stepped out onto the swept concrete floor, heard Tom do the same behind him. The only lighting was provided by two burning torches, both attached to stanchions on the wall. And the white walls held no decoration save for one age-weathered portrait of an old white haired woman sitting in a rocker. In her lap, a cat slept beneath the woman's knitting. Her eyes were cut out.

Mathis walked up to the portrait, the rubber soles of his Bostonian Blues clacking on the clean concrete. "Why the hell you figure someone'd do something like cut an old lady's eyes out?"

Someone answered, and it wasn't Tom. "Because history is blind...and we all need the reminder."

Heart leaping in chest, Mathis turned toward the voice. A man stood in the only doorway, dark eyes recessed into his head like little chunks of coal inside a snowball. Mathis also noticed a slightly distended belly pushing through a light-blue work shirt, like the man enjoyed his food. The nameplate read, "Eric." The thinning red hair and the thin grin, which seemed little more than a parting of the guy's nearly bloodless lips, served in no way to help Mathis assess the man's age.

Mathis had no idea what the man meant. "Why are you using torches? Have you no electricity?" But he knew this was absurd. The factory had to have electricity to run. He knew damn well receiving and shipping had electricity aplenty.

"Fire's cheaper," the man said quietly, like it should've been obvious.

Confused, and strangely frightened, Mathis glance darted back to the picture. The old woman looked familiar, he now noticed. He should know her.

Tom must've noticed Mathis staring intently. "Gladys," he said. "Her name's Gladys and she used to work in hardware. You know, before..."

"Before the Testament of the Union," Eric whispered. "She now dines at the feast of the divine. She is the first, but more will follow."

"What the hell is the 'feast of the divine'?" Mathis asked.

"The sacrifice to the gods within," Eric said. He sounded dead, his voice a liquid gurgle. "They bless us with resources."

"What kind of resources?" Mathis felt Tom backing away slowly, like he might try to bolt.

"Human—and otherwise," Eric said. "What we need for efficiency."

"But—but Petersheim performs work based on results, not efficiencies," Mathis reminded him.

"We are of the Testament of the Union," Eric said like a zombie.

Mathis puffed up his chest, intending to look authoritative. "We want to know why there are blood stains on our product. It's happening inside your sealed facility."

Eric looked puzzled for a moment. He tipped his head sideways as though listening to someone Mathis couldn't hear. "The product is not our concern, only the machines and building."

"But your machines build the product."

"I don't think he cares," Tom whispered from somewhere behind Mathis.

After a while the man said, "The product is not defective. Some clean-up must be expected." Now he sounded like a robot, Mathis thought, like Eric just regurgitated somebody else's words.

"I demand to speak to your supervisor," Mathis said, voice raised. He could hear his own fear reflected in it and that made him more nervous.

"As you wish," Eric said, his monotone voice barely audible. "Follow me. Don't forget, safety first."

Mathis followed Eric through a wide doorway. He heard Tom's tentative steps behind them. From the bit of light available, Mathis could see they now stood on top of metal grating—the floor of an upper-level mezzanine if Mathis remembered correctly. Then the door slammed shut behind them, as if on its own accord, plunging them into complete darkness.

"Where are all the lights?" Tom howled, his voice shrill.

"The use of light is inefficient," Eric droned in the darkness. "Follow me."

Shallow clunks descending told Mathis that Eric was walking downstairs. He struggled to find the handrail and then followed the man down. He heard Tom hesitate, but then reluctantly follow. The footsteps reverberated around the facility as if they were inside a huge cave. When they reached the bottom, the now concrete floor sounded quieter than the metal.

Mathis heard the furtive scurrying of several feet, somewhere off to his left. Then the shrill cry of a baby broke the silence.

"What's that?" Tom cried out. Then, "Ouch, someone shoved me."

Mathis felt someone take hold of his shoulders with strong ice-like fingers. Those fingers began to guide him. He tried to break the grip but couldn't.

"Those are future resources," Eric said as if nothing out of the usual was happening.

"Future resources?" Mathis asked. He made one more feeble and unsuccessful attempt at breaking away. It was like being held by iron shackles.

"Of course," Eric said. "We are a self-contained maintenance system. Nobody enters, nobody leaves."

"But we entered," Mathis said. Oh how he now wished they hadn't. Flashes of his patient wife sifted through his mind like a slideshow. He strained to hear Tom breathe but couldn't.

"Of course," Eric said. "That is sometimes necessary for the integration of fresh resources—and for the offering."

"Offering to whom?" Mathis said. "And where is your supervisor?"

"The gods within," he said, as if the two questions had the same answer. "The gods within the Testament of the Union."

"Show me," Mathis demanded.

"As you wish," Eric said.

Silently, several torches sprang to life, their flames starting red and dull then rising into bright blue spears. Mathis gasped.

He tried to see who held him but couldn't. Then he concentrated on the vision before him. Obviously the self-contained maintenance system had gone awry.

Directly before him, a giant black conveyor belt labored under the weight of several door sections, all lazily making their way toward shipping as if on a stroll down a calm river. Above the conveyer hung a cross, and on the cross a withered corpse. The eyes within the ancient skull had long since withered to dust, old clothes hanging in tatters from the mummified body. Old white hair clung to the back of the cranium like a mullet. Mathis knew it was Gladys. Next to her hung several other corpses that Mathis thought he should recognize.

"These are your gods?" Mathis asked. "They're just old employees."

"The gods within," Eric corrected. "They demand regeneration and blood."

"What do you mean?" Mathis asked.

"You are fit," Eric said. "You shall help regenerate the system with your fresh seed." As if on cue, several figures shambled into the light of the torches. All with white, translucent skin and filmy white eyes, some were women, some men, but all clothed in the blue uniforms of the Union. A couple of the women carried babies. "And when you have reached your end," Eric continued, "so shall you also take your place among the gods within."

As Eric spoke, words Mathis barely heard, Tom was hoisted quietly upward. The cord around his throat stifled his screams. When the cord tightened, Tom's eyes bulged, then his blood released—appeasing the gods within, Mathis knew—and sprayed the host of decaying flesh.

Mathis couldn't help but notice that some of the blood seeped to the doors on the conveyor as they made their idle way to shipping.

THE WILD HUNT
Sarah Glenn Marsh

I.
DANIEL

The old man glares at us from beside the open mouth of the grave.

"Watch where you're going!" he rasps, leaning against his tall shovel. His washed-out eyes narrow farther as Matt and I stop mid-run, kicking some dirt into the grave this old guy's been digging.

"Sorry," I pant, flicking sweat off my forehead. I'm so hot from the run, I don't mind the late October chill or the steely sky above the little cemetery. "We're on the track team at Bellmont High, and we've got a meet coming up, so—"

"You're using the path through the woods for practice. I know. I used to be a coach at Bellmont." The old guy's teeth are mottled yellow and black, kind of like the colored corn my mom likes to hang on our front door in the fall. "But tonight's Halloween. Don't you have anything better to do?"

This old man's probably a pedophile. Matt looks at me and shrugs, then glances at the gravedigger. "There's the trick-or-treat scavenger hunt tonight." He coughs, and I shake my head, hoping he'll realize we need to get going.

But Matt's not the brightest. It's why I usually avoid him outside of practices.

"The hunt actually starts around here," he adds, his voice gravelly as the gravedigger's now. "Whoever figures out the clues finds their way to a crazy party."

The old guy grins, showing off his nasty teeth. "Sounds like a wild time." He reaches for something in his pocket, and I tense. If he tries anything freaky, I'll run like hell.

But he just shows Matt a couple cough drops that look like they've been in his pocket for a hundred years. "Want one?" After Matt grabs a few, he offers them to me, slowly blinking those faded eyes. I take one, just to be polite.

Poor, harmless weirdo.

"Every grave tells a story, you know," the old man says. He gazes across the cemetery, still leaning on his shovel. "Why don't you stay awhile? I feel like sharing a tale or two with some young blood."

I beat Matt to answering. "We actually need to head home and shower before tonight. Thanks though."

"Just one story," the old guy begs.

Matt nods, coughing again. I cross my arms and sigh, but I don't take off without him.

I'm a saint.

II.

MELISSA

The scream could've come from anywhere.

Dead husks crunch under my feet as I race around the fringes of the little graveyard, trying to spot the source of the awful noise. Trouble is, Bell's Wood surrounds the weed-choked cemetery on all sides, and everything looks the same at night.

Heart lodged in my throat, I fumble for the pocket knife in my front pocket. Stupid tight jeans. It takes a minute, but I finally pull it free as the scream comes again, loud enough to rip leaves off the trees.

Closer. Stronger. Making the branches shiver.

The sound of my heart drowns out the worst of the shrieking as I squint into the darkness. If my hands don't stop shaking, my knife won't be much use.

My shoulders slump as five familiar figures burst through a gap in the trees. Three of them are lanky shadows with broad shoulders, and they laugh as they chase two smaller shadows between moon-washed gravestones.

Finally, my friends are here. They gather around me, panting, winded, but grinning wider than the pumpkins we carved this afternoon.

"Jerks." I take a deep breath and glare. "What took you so long?"

Veronica tosses her sheet of dark hair over her shoulder and flashes a smile. "Relax, Mel," she drawls. She's lived here for over a year, but her Southern accent hasn't yet succumbed to the crispness of northern Massachusetts. "We just had a hard time pickin' what to wear for our trick-or-treat adventure."

She loops a bare arm around Ally's shoulders. Both of them must be freezing in their sequined tops and tiny ruffled skirts. I can't tell what they're supposed to be, though Ally's got calico cat ears pinned to her pale hair.

Over in the graveyard, Jason, Luke, and Wes are already exploring.

"You two realize this is a scavenger hunt, right?" I cram the knife back in my pocket as my friends shiver so hard their heads bang together. They stumble apart, laughing, leading me to wonder how much they've already had to drink. "We're gonna be crawling through the dark, muddy woods searching for clues until we find the seniors' lame Halloween party."

Veronica and Ally both frown, but I don't care. They kept me waiting in the cold for nearly an hour.

"And someone told me," I continue, "the abandoned house they're using for the party won't be there much longer—the fire department's using it for a practice burn this winter. It's probably full of bugs and mold."

Still frowning, Ally rubs one of her glitter-dusted cheeks. The flecks scatter like falling stars. "We don't mind the mud. That's why we wore these." She points at her laced-up boots, like that solves everything. "Besides, we know how to keep warm."

The flask she pulls from Veronica's oversized handbag gleams brighter than the headstones where the guys are prowling for clues.

For a moment, I think of the bodies below those stones, nestled deep in the earth, slowly crumbling to nothing as time forgets them and weather erases their names. I wonder if they mind the stench of sixteen-year-old boy sweat and the gag-inducing fumes from Jason's cigarette.

Veronica waves a hand in front of my face. "Is that really what you're wearin'? A t-shirt and jeans?"

All thoughts of the graveyard's inhabitants vanish as I meet her disapproving gaze.

"Yeah." I square my shoulders. "So? I don't want to get scratched. And this is festive." I pat the silhouette of a witch on the front of my long-sleeved tee.

"All right." Veronica shrugs, then drops her voice. "I just thought you'd want Wes to see you in somethin' a little more *interesting* tonight. After all, it's Halloween. The one night you can be somebody else…like, I dunno, the kind of girl who goes out with a hottie like Wes." She flicks her brown eyes toward the graveyard.

Ally clumsily pats my back. "There's always next year." Her breath reeks of cheap rum. "Then we'll be the seniors throwing the party. And *I'll* choose your costume."

"Hey!" Luke's waving to us. Something white dangles from one of his hands: our first scavenger hunt clue. It must've been somewhere in the graveyard. "You three wanna talk all night, or can we go find this damn party?"

Wes leads the way into the inky blackness of the trees, visible only by the dancing beam of his flashlight. Luke and Veronica follow him, holding hands. I go next, with Jason on my heels, puffing away at the glowing stub of his last cigarette. Ally stumbles behind us, flask in hand.

"What'd the clue say?" I call softly. We've left it where we found it, just like we were told, so others on the hunt will have a fair chance.

"Shhhhh," Veronica hisses. "Do you want every junior at Bellmont to know the way because we did all the work for 'em?"

Pausing by a twisted oak tree, Wes lets Luke and Veronica amble ahead, passing them the flashlight. As I join him, he puts his lips to my ear and whispers, "I forget the words, but I think we're supposed to follow this trail to a waterfall." He holds out his hand and grins. "Walk with me? We should use the buddy system…"

"Yeah. Sounds good." Warmth shoots up my arm as we link fingers.

We trail a good distance from the others. Despite the absence of light, Wes seems sure of the way, so I stick close to his side.

I wonder who started the tradition of a Halloween scavenger hunt through Bell's Wood. The funny thing is, I'm sure someone explained it just the other day. I can't remember who told us all to meet at the graveyard, either. The whole day's a blur.

I guess being close to Wes has that effect on me.

"Sweet!" Luke's voice bounces off the trees. I'm pretty sure the harsh shushing that follows is Veronica.

We take a few more steps before I see the flashlight's weak beam spilling across damp earth. Ducking under a branch that rakes my hair like grasping fingers, I finally hear another noise over the rustling of nighttime creatures: the pulse of water pummeling large stones.

"Look," Veronica breathes, holding up a clear plastic bag of candy. Someone's scrawled the words *Help Yourselves* across it in Sharpie.

Ally, Wes, and I join Veronica and Luke as they untie the bag, but Jason hangs back, finishing his cig. He smothers the glowing embers with the heel of his boot, and the woods get that much blacker.

Laughing, Luke pulls a fistful of candy from the bag. "Who's hungry?" Kneeling by the flashlight, he unwraps a couple of sour balls in shades of lurid green, shiny plastic red, and neon yellow. They look more fake than Ally's nose.

"Me! Me!" Veronica crouches next to Luke, and I look away as he starts popping candy in her mouth. After all, we're not supposed to throw up *before* the party. But the sound of her sucking on his fingers makes my stomach churn.

"Well, isn't this a night of thrills," Jason grumbles. He's watching the small waterfall and crinkling a butterscotch wrapper like he wishes he'd brought more cigarettes. "Don't you want some candy?" He winks at me, pops the butterscotch in his mouth, and shatters it with his teeth.

I shake my head, but I'm glad for the distraction. "I'm holding out for something with chocolate. Was the next clue in the bag?"

"It's right here!" Ally totters over with the flask in one hand and a white slip of paper in the other. Her cat ears are lopsided.

As I lean in for a look at the clue, a gust of hot air on the back of my neck sends me scrambling toward Jason.

"Easy, Mel!" Wes holds up his hands to show he hadn't meant to startle me, and heat rises in my cheeks.

Ally unfolds the paper. "Over the river and through the woods, to the Fun House we go…"

"The river. Huh." Wes scrubs a hand over his shadowed jaw. "I don't know of any river around here, but if we head east a while, this stream gets wider. Maybe we're supposed to cross there?"

I nod, Ally takes a sip from the flask, and Jason shrugs. "Whatever, man."

As Wes picks up the flashlight, Veronica hurries over to us, frowning. "You guys go on without us. Luke's got a bad stomach ache. Must've been the burgers from dinner."

"What?" Ally pouts. "You can't be serious."

Veronica's brows knit together. For a second, she looks paler than I've ever seen her. Must be the moonlight. "I am serious. Ya'll have fun. Dance on some tables for me."

As she hurries back to Luke, a horrible retching noise comes from beside the waterfall. So they aren't just ditching us to make out.

"Come on," Jason mutters, taking the flashlight and charging ahead. This time, I grab Wes's hand before he can offer it. We follow Ally and Jason down a leaf-trampled rut that passes for a trail.

Aside from the crunching our feet make as we trudge eastward, following the stream, the woods are oddly hushed. There're no squirrels scurrying up the trees anymore. There's no wind, just frigid air, making my nose prickle with numbness.

Worst of all is the pins-and-needles feeling that starts in my fingertips and spreads up my arms, into my chest, and then to my head.

Where are all the other drunk juniors who're supposed to be swarming the woods, looking for the party? It doesn't feel like we've been walking long, but maybe we've gone too far the wrong way.

"That's it." Jason stops abruptly in the middle of the path, and Ally staggers to avoid bumping into him. "I'm gonna find Luke and Veronica. Make sure Luke's doing okay. I mean, I drove them to the cemetery, so they need a ride home."

He's rubbing his throat. He must really want to get back to his car, where I'll bet there's a new pack of cigarettes waiting.

"Take the flashlight," Wes offers. "We'll manage without."

Jason runs a hand through his slicked-back hair before waving away the offer. "Nah. I'll be fine."

As he lowers his hand, my gaze catches on his throat. There's a spot over his Adam's apple as dark as a blackberry stain, and it appears to spread down his chest, the color stark against his white shirt collar. "Later, guys."

"Wait!" I shout. With every step, his shadowy figure looks a little less solid, a little greyer. Like he's walking into a thick fog. "Jason, something's wrong!" He doesn't pause, so I dash after him. "Jason!"

The outlines of crooked trees are visible through his retreating form. I shut my eyes, and when I open them a moment later, he's gone. So is the thin mist into which he vanished. Shivering, I strain to listen for footsteps. Nothing. No owls, no shouts from distant scavenger hunters.

"Let him go, Mel," Wes calls. He wouldn't be saying that if he'd seen the stain on Jason's throat, or that weird mist.

Swallowing hard, I rejoin the dwindling group. I just want to go home. I don't know what I saw, or whether I'm imagining things. Maybe I've been out in the cold too long. Or maybe— no. That has to be it.

"What's going on?" Ally whines, tucking her shaking hands in the crooks of her elbows. "I just wanna get to the party."

When we finally get close enough to hear the *whoosh* of the widening stream, Ally spots the next bag of candy between two boulders on the other side. With a tense smile, Wes helps Ally cross, using the rocks as stepping stones.

Guess I'm last. I put a foot on the flattest rock in sight, testing to make sure it isn't too slippery Stepping into the stream, I shudder as icy water floods my sneakers.

"I'm starving," Ally says from the rocky stream bank. Her words are followed by the crinkling of another candy bag.

I'm almost across. Two more rocks and I'll be scrambling up the bank.

As I balance between the stones, sounds of choking split the air. I glance up and almost fall. Wes is bending over Ally. Is she having a seizure? Her body's writhing like she's in shock. Is he starting CPR? I don't think she can breathe. I can't, either.

Something's really wrong.

I slide and flail my arms, fighting to regain balance.

"Melissa." Wes's voice strains. "She's not—not breathing. Nothing I do is helping. She choked on that damn candy!" He covers his face with his hands, shaking. "I don't know what else to do. Oh, God, I can't…"

Finally, I make it to the last rock. I cross to the boulders where Wes is still crouching with his head in his hands, but there's no sign of Ally sprawled in front of him. Just the open candy bag. My breath hitches.

"Where is she?"

First Jason, now Ally. What's in these woods that can make people disappear?

Wes lowers his hands. "What? She was right—" He stares at the spot where he'd been hovering over Ally.

It takes a moment to unstick my tongue from my bone-dry mouth. "Read the clue."

"What?"

"Read the next clue," I say, more sure of myself. "We have to find the party and get help!" Wes is staring at the peanut butter cups scattered around the boulders. "*Now!*"

He reads the clue, but I don't hear it. I'm glancing between trees, hoping to spot a flash of pale hair and cat ears. When Wes pulls me up a hill and along a new path, I realize we're circling back to the west, but I don't complain. If we end up back at the cemetery instead of at the party, we can drive to the police station.

Sure enough, as we emerge from a stand of narrow trees, familiar headstones glowing softly in the moonlight welcome us back to the graveyard. And at the base of a stunted tree, just before the cemetery's low gate, is the next bag of candy.

Wes collapses next to the bag, shaking harder than he was back at the stream.

"What's wrong now?" I ask, not really wanting an answer.

The bag crinkles as Wes tears the plastic apart and shoves a hand into the candy. "Low blood sugar," he manages between stuffing red and purple sweets in his mouth. "Gimme a minute."

I crouch beside him, watching him inhale a couple of candies. There are a few foil-wrapped chocolates among the gummy worms. *Finally*. I push a piece of chocolate past my lips, then another. I hadn't realized how hungry I was.

With the next piece I take, I grab a slip of white paper. The final clue. Heat spreads through me, and my shoulders sag with relief. Maybe everything will be fine in the morning. Wes and I will find the party, we'll check on our friends, and then we'll have a great time. Maybe we'll even kiss.

"You're almost there, but not quite here yet," the paper reads. I think. The words run together before my tired eyes.

I try to ask Wes what he thinks, but my hand is suddenly too heavy to pass him the paper. And when I look at the spot where he was sitting, it's empty. There's not even a patch of crushed leaves to show he was ever there.

The pleasant warmth of the chocolate becomes a burn in my throat. I can't move my tongue. I can't shout for Wes. My heart hammers in my ears so hard, I think it's going to burst. There's something wet dribbling from my lips. Please be spit. Not blood. Please.

I can't look.

The little cemetery shimmers under my blurry gaze, and then—

A house appears, just beyond the gravestones. It's an old colonial, its white paint chipped in places, backing up to the woods. Every light in the house is on, and I realize I can see clearly again as I pick out the shadows of guys and girls dancing inside. Music pulses through the windows, calling me closer, and my heart matches its rhythm.

I'll get help there.

Staggering to my feet, which is easier than I expected, I run across the graveyard and try the door without knocking.

"Hey, gorgeous." Wes stands in the foyer, a beer in one hand and an orange-and-black paper streamer draped around his shoulders.

"Where the hell have you been? I was so scared. I couldn't find you!" I don't realize I've shouted until everyone in the house turns to me. There's Luke and Veronica tangled up together, seeming annoyed by the distraction. There's Jason, taking a drag from a cigarette. There's Ally, dancing with two other girls from my literature class. Half the football team is here too, stuffing their faces with cake and chips.

"Answer me," I choke out, and Wes frowns. His lips are blue. Everyone's lips are blue. The stain on Jason's throat is darker than berry juice. The football players have them, too. Everyone does. And, I note with a thrill of horror as I look into the heavy oval mirror in the hallway, so do I.

There's blood and chocolate on my t-shirt. The candy. *It was poisoned*. It must've been. And that means everyone in this house—everyone dancing in their bloody clothes, laughing with blue lips, and kissing each other's bruised throats—they're dead.

I sink to the floor with a dull thud as my head spins. *I'm* dead.

III.
DANIEL

"They never found the killer," the old man says, gazing into the freshly dug grave with something like longing. "But every Halloween night, I hear the ghosts of those kids out in the woods, reliving their final hours."

I glance from the gravedigger to the headstones at his back. *Melissa Reyes. Ally Lawson. Wesley Tillman.* Those poor kids. I had no idea. I can't believe people still hold the scavenger hunt every year, two decades later.

"Time to go," I snap at Matt. "Seriously, come on."

When his eyes meet mine, I realize they look glassy. He chokes, clawing at his throat.

Instead of helping him, I take a step back. The funny thing is, my throat's really tight, too. "What—what are those graves for?" I gasp.

The old man smiles and laughs. His teeth aren't just yellow, I see now. They're curved and sharp as a wolf's fangs.

CORRUPT

Kim Graff

D AD CUT MOM'S HEART OUT and put it in a jar over the
fireplace. Sometimes I wish he hadn't, but for the most
part it doesn't really matter. You need a father to learn
how to be a man and I don't remember what it was like when she
was here, so there's really not a whole lot to miss. It's not like it
was his fault, Mom should've known better than to go outside.

Our cabin is the only safe haven left in this world, leaving
it is as good as slitting your own wrists. Outside, the forest
surrounded us, filled with savages. Dad's the only one who can
cross the threshold and come back untainted. He foraged for our
food and collected water from the stream behind our cabin. I've
heard it, the water trickling down over the rocks, but never seen
it. All of our windows are boarded up; if it weren't for books, I
wouldn't know what the outside world used to look like.

Dad always said it was too dangerous to even take a peek,
but Mom didn't listen. She left one day when it was taking Dad

too long to find herbs for my fever, became corrupted, and had to die. She should've known better.

She wasn't the first Corrupt I'd seen, and I doubt she'd be the last. Dad found them out in the woods. He'd bring them back bound and gagged to keep them from spewing their lies or infecting us. Two would go down to the cellar. One would return. Sometimes I'd hear screams, never from Dad, and that'd be that. I'd never see the Corrupt again.

We didn't talk about it, but I knew we were the only Pure left.

Most my time was spent smothering my fear and reasoning away every sound. The branches breaking in the forest were always just animals. The flutter of the bushes: *animals*. During the day, that was easy enough. But when the sun disappeared behind the tall trees, when the shadows crawled out into our small clearing, when we had nothing but candles to keep the night away….

In my dreams, every floorboard creak, every twig snap, was a Corrupt coming closer.

One day, twenty hours, and forty-five minutes was the longest Dad had ever been gone before. This time—three days, four hours, and seventeen minutes—was nearly twice that. Something had to be wrong.

Even though it went against Dad's advice, I pulled a board down from the window to look out. Dawn had just started to break in its ugly shade of orange, like fire spreading through the sky. The sun wasn't high over the treetops brightening the forest. Shadows still ruled the ground.

There was still no sign of Dad. I gnawed at my lower lip as I walked to the front door. A thousand things could go wrong if I went outside, but … Dad had never been gone this long before, and wouldn't a man go outside? Fight for his family? It sounded like something Dad would say.

With a deep breath, I calmed the quiver in my heart and grabbed the same sort of gear Dad always did before one of his trips. I stuffed a jug of water, loaf of stale bread, one box of bullets into a spare duffle bag and heaved it over my shoulder. Two boards barricaded the door. If I went outside, no one would be left here to lock it. The cabin could be compromised. Our *only* safe haven.

I shouldn't go. This place was my home, I couldn't remember a life before here, but was it really home without Dad? Eventually I'd have to go out and hunt for food. I shifted my feet as I looked at the door. *But Dad could come back...*

Or he could be hurt out there, waiting for me to come save him.

"Screw it," I said as I pulled the boards free and opened the door.

I gripped the duffle bag tighter as I looked at the ground. Tentatively, I stepped out onto the dirt path, testing the ground before I put all my weight onto it. Like somehow it wouldn't hold me, and I'd get swallowed up into a void of nothing.

Don't be stupid. I shook those frightened, *childish* thoughts from my mind as I closed the door behind me. I paused at the edge of the clearing, where I'd have to enter the forest to go any further.

Shadows cast the forest into darkness. I couldn't see any threats, any Corrupts, until I ventured in. Maybe I was waiting for a better idea. Or at least until it was more light. Dad would be back. Probably with a sack filled with deer meat slung over his shoulders, enough to feed us for weeks. The Corrupt couldn't get him.

I couldn't survive if he was gone.

No, no. I had to be a man. I forced myself to enter the forest, to go fast and through it, dodging the shadows and staying in what little light cascaded through the treetops. It wasn't until I was too far in that I realized what a horrible idea it was. I didn't know the forest like Dad. Everything looked the same; all I could do was keep going straight, north, toward the mountains like Dad had. That way, if I had to turn around, I should've been able to find my way home. Dad needed me. Bad idea or not, I had to do this. To be a man.

The forest went on forever now, Dad told me so, but I was hoping to find another cabin or clearing. Somewhere Dad might've camped out if he ran into trouble. *Crunch.* I froze. The sound came from behind me, to the left, but I didn't move. Couldn't even breathe. If I stood still, whatever was there wouldn't notice me … right? *Crack.* Don't breathe.

Don't. Breathe.

A stampede of footsteps rushed toward me. I leapt into the closest bush—one filled with prickling thorns that tore my sleeves. The thorns might keep the Corrupt away. When I looked out, it was a just a deer. Standing where I once stood, looking in the opposite direction of me. I let out my breath slowly. It wasn't until it had walked away that I pried myself free of the thorn bush and began my trek again, thankful that Dad hadn't seen me panic. He would've thought it pathetic. I hadn't even tried to kill it like he would've.

Sixteen-years-old and afraid of a deer, some man I'd turned out to be...

Twelve feet ahead, I could see the trees break into a clearing. When I got to the edge, I hid behind a thick tree to survey the area. The ground was unlike anything I'd ever seen before. The clearing was about twenty feet, ten of which consisted of a strip of blackness. It looked a little like a river of thick, black, dried mud. I glanced both ways before emerging from the trees to walk up to the path. I placed a foot on it and pressed down. It was solid.

I took another step on it.

A screaming unlike anything I'd ever heard ripped through the air. I stumbled back, placing my hands over my ears. A red metal thing zoomed by me, heading on the black strip with such speed.

My breath quickened as I followed the direction the red box disappeared into. Just over a hill, I could see where it was most likely heading. There was a cluster of buildings below. Some were tall, more than just a story, and few the color of wood. It didn't make sense. If I ever came across another place, I expected it to be abandoned or frantic with Corrupt. Yet, as I looked down onto the area, I could see people walking around who looked fairly normal. No one was running around like crazed creatures. There were a lot more metal boxes—*cars*, I remembered them from my books—moving around as well.

Was Dad there? Did he finally find more Pure? But … if we were so close to this place, how could he never have found it before?

"What do you think of this new fella, Roosevelt?" An old man asked, holding a big piece of flappy paper. I could only read one part, which was written bigger than the rest: FRANKLIN D. ROOSEVELT ELECTED PRESIDENT.

"Don't blow your wig over him," the other man said with a grunt.

I didn't understand. I really didn't—I wandered the town until the sun disappeared, listening and watching those around me. They all sounded … normal. Looked normal. They didn't seem too happy, these people, but they weren't devouring each other or anything. I sorta expected that type of behavior from the Corrupt. Is this a trick? Are they trying to lull me into a false sense of … something? But why?

This was an illusion. It had got to be. A dream even, maybe?

Someone tapped my shoulder. I leapt and tripped over my feet when I turned, almost falling into the girl in front of me.

"Hello, stranger," she said. She brushed a strand of her black hair behind her ears and let her greener-than-grass eyes wash over me. "I've seen you walking around all afternoon. You lookin' for something in particular? I might be able to help."

She talked. That shouldn't have surprised me. The other people talked too, but she … she sounded different than the others. Her voice was soft like a flower's petal and sweet like its nectar.

"Hello?" Her eyes stopped on my waist—the left side. I knew what she was looking at. My dad's spare gun. I turned so she couldn't see it anymore.

"That's a hot piece. You a trigger man or somethin'? Searching for your target to kill for your boss? Are you in the mob? I've never met someone like that before. Those types of people usually stay in the Big Apple. At least I thought so. You look too young to be a trigger man."

"Trigger man? I don't know what that means," I said. She talked weirdly—everyone did. "Where am I?"

"Where … are you?" She tilted her head. "Are you funny in the head? I kinda thought so, just watching you and all."

"Who are you?"

She smiled. "Winifred. Friends call me Winnie. Who're you?"

"Corwin." There was a pause, as if she was waiting for something else. I didn't know what to do—or say—so I went with the truth. At least the closest thing I knew to it. My name was really Corwin Jr., but my dad just called me Junior. For some reason, I didn't want this girl to do the same.

A huge smile broke out across her face. "Cor*win* and *Winn*ie. How perfect is that?"

I didn't get it. My confusion gave way a little to something else, something warm, just watching her be so cheery. The way her freckles crinkled around her nose when she smiled was somehow appealing.

"I'm real confused," I said. "I ... I'm looking for my dad. He came this way three days ago. I haven't seen him since."

A gleam came into her eyes. "Ah, so your *dad's* in the mob. You're just looking for him?"

"What? No. What's with you and mobs? What's a mob?"

She shrugged her shoulder. "I've always wanted to be a moll—"

"A *what*?"

Winnie paused, stared at me, then dragged her hand across her face. "Lord, don't you know anything? A moll — a gangster's girl. These days, they've got it all. The mob still has money, plenty of food — their girls get to dress nice, go to parties, have fun. So you're really not a trigger man?"

"I'm really not. I just want to find my dad."

"Did he come this way for work? 'Cause I can tell ya' now, there ain't none."

I shook my head. "Food, supplies, stuff like that."

"Barely any of that either," she said as she turned on her heels and started to walk away. After a few steps, she glanced back at me. "Well, you coming?"

Apparently, I was.

"This here is Corwin," Winnie announced after we entered a house. It was one of the rundown shed-sized places on the edge of the town. There was a group of kids around our age, all doing a whole lot of nothing. "Found him wandering around town. He's from the Big Apple, looking for his dad."

Some looked up at me, others didn't bother.

"Hear about Becky?" asked one of the girls on the couch.

"Hear what?" Winnie walked through the trash and sat on the only open seat. I didn't want to get any closer. What if one was infected? What if just by being here meant I was infected? I didn't really know how it worked, since Dad never explained it to me. We were Pure, the ones he brought back were the Corrupt. It was our job to get rid of as many as possible. Dad even said when he got back from his trip this time, I'd get to help him with his work down in the cellar.

What if this is what happened with Mom? People tricked her into thinking they were okay, and then *bang* she was tainted. Would Dad cut my heart out too?

"Becky's gone," the little girl said.

Winnie frowned. "You sure?"

"Sure as sure gets."

Winnie looked down to her hands. After a moment's pause, she began to pick the dirt out from under her nails. "That's too bad, I liked Becky."

"She's… what? The fifth in the last three months?" one of the smaller boys said. "Ain't no one notice all these girls going missin'? My mom used to say it's been happening for ages. Why don't someone do something about it? Where's the coppers when you need 'em?"

This got my attention—girls going missing, that sounded *just* like something a Corrupt would do. Maybe these people were all ignorant. Maybe that's why Dad and I were Pures—we knew about the problem, we tried to fix it, while these ignorants sat around doing nothing all day.

"Who's to say they didn't just leave town?" Winnie asked. "Becky's been talking about going to the Apple for ages. She thought she could get on Broadway or something. Become someone. Told her it was a bad idea, but I guess she went anyway."

"You don't think anything's happened to her?"

"I doubt anything good'll happen to her," Winnie said. "Nothing good happens to anyone anymore."

Still, none of what they said mattered to me. Finding Dad had to be my priority, then we'd maybe help out with the missing girl problem. I turned around and walked out the door. Someone shouted my name in the house, probably Winnie, but I didn't stop. When I got to the end of her street, she caught up with me.

"What're you doing?"

"I'm looking for my dad."

"But it'll get dark soon, you should just stay with us for the night. It's not safe out here at night."

Now that got my attention. I turned back to her. "Why?"

"There's something … out there," she said in a small voice. "Sometimes when people go wandering around at night, they don't come back. These are bad times, Corwin. You shouldn't have to be alone during bad times."

My heart shivered. Dad. What if he was the one who wasn't going to come back? Winnie seemed to know what I was thinking, because her frown got all the bigger. "Sorry, Corwin.… Please come back with me. Just 'til morning light."

"I—I've got to find my dad."

"I'll help you look tomorrow, 'kay? I promise."

There wasn't enough room at the house for everyone to have a place for himself. Three to five kids slept in each room, including the kitchen. I didn't bother to talk to most, but that didn't stop them from talking to me. Some of their dads went to other towns looking for work, and then their moms vanished into the nights. Others lost their parents to starvation or disease and had nowhere left to go. But no one talked of the Corrupt.

Yet.

Winnie let me share her sheets to stay warm. She also didn't bother me with questions like the others. From what I could gather, she was the ringleader of this pack. The house was her family's. Winnie took the others in when they had nowhere else to go. She and the older kids searched for work and food, a way to feed everyone.

Like Winnie promised, we went around town looking for my dad the next day. I realized it was pointless, that my dad wasn't there. If he were, I'd have found him already. There were a hundred different ways he could've gone when he left the cabin, and I was pretty sure that this wasn't the way. I told her as much, so she took me back to the edge of town.

"You sure you want to leave?"

"I am," I said. I'd head back to our cabin — I was pretty sure I could find the way — and if Dad wasn't there, I'd try another direction.

"It's dangerous out there," she said.

"It's dangerous everywhere."

She didn't argue with that. Instead, she grabbed my shoulders and got up on her tiptoes to press her lips against mine. I didn't know what to do, to say, in return.

"Who knows, with times like these," Winnie said and shrugged. "What's going to happen, I could be dead tomorrow. At least today I can say I've finally kissed a boy."

"All … right." That didn't seem like enough, but saying thank you seemed wrong too.

"Junior!"

I froze. That voice. I looked behind us and saw Dad there, in his hunter's gear, a bow over his shoulders. His face covered in a four-day beard. His eyes stuck on Winnie.

"Dad!"

"What are you doing out?" he said with such anger—I had never heard him talk like that before.

"You were gone for so long. I didn't know—"

He strode right pass me to Winnie. The next thing I knew, he smacked her. She fell limp, so he grabbed her and put her over his shoulder. Without another word, he started to head toward the forest.

"What're you doing—?"

"Silence. Follow."

I didn't know what to do as Dad hauled Winnie into the forest.

"Dad, what—?"

"You let her touch you! You want to get infected? Let her corrupt you? Like your mother did?" he asked.

"I—"

"Silence, Junior."

Dad … I had never heard him so angry — not at me, at least. He'd use this voice whenever he ranted about the Corrupt, about how they ruined the world for everyone else. How Mom should've listened to him, shouldn't have left us. If she didn't, if she stayed like she promised, she'd be alive still. He wouldn't have had to do what he did.

It was her fault. Not his.

Winnie began to stir as soon as we got near the cabin. I'd been watching her closely on the trek back, hoping he hadn't hit her hard enough to do serious damage. Then again, I sorta did. Nothing good would happen once Dad got her to cellar; it might've been better for her to not ever wake up again.

Her eyes blinked open, slowly at first, then she seemed to realize what was happening. Those green, green eyes of hers widened as she glanced around. I wanted to shrink away when they landed on me.

"Corwin, help me!"

"Silence," Dad said as he jerked her hard enough her head whipped to the side. She closed her eyes tight and started muttering something—a prayer, maybe, but I hadn't heard one of those since Mom died.

Dad was the first one in the cabin. Like all the other times, he went straight down to the cellar with his Corrupt. Instead of closing the door right behind him, though, he left it wide opened.

I froze. This was the moment I'd been waiting for my whole life. To be able to be just like him—to help him with his work.

The mason jar on the mantel stole my attention. Dad said he put it there, Mom's heart, as a reminder of the dangers outside. To show me what could be tainted if I stepped out of line.

Mom was the first Corrupt to go down in the cellar. Or maybe I was too young to remember any before. I had been playing in the main area, trying not to think too hard about the fact I was all by myself, when Dad burst in through the door. Mom was slung over his shoulder, mouth gagged, hands tied.

When I started to cry, Dad told me to be quiet or *else*. Mom pleaded with her eyes—her green, bright eyes—and I shut up.

They went down to the cellar. I never saw her again.

The cellar was a dank, dark place with nothing but a table and a case filled with jars, just like the one up on the mantel. These were the hearts of other Corrupts. Winnie was tied down to the long table in the center of the room. There was rope attached to every leg of the table. Red flakes of dried blood covered everything. Winnie's screaming died when Dad gagged her.

Her green eyes shot to me. Pleading just like Mom's did.

"Dad. I don't think ... I mean, she's not like the others. She's different—"

"She's corrupted. They're *all* corrupt. We must not let them corrupt us. Do you understand, son?"

"She's just a girl—she's normal. She was helping me find you—"

"You will not argue with me! Do you not see how she has corrupted you already? Where did your *disrespect* come from?"

Was he right? I had never questioned him before—never had to rethink his actions. Now ... now there was doubt. Was that Winnie's fault? He took out a knife from his belt and held it out to me.

"We must destroy all the Corrupt, Junior."

I looked at the knife, then at Winnie.

Her green eyes were so bright I feared their power would melt me. I had never before questioned Dad. Never had such doubt in me. Was that her fault? The world was horrible out there, I'd seen it with my own eyes. All those people were suffering, and maybe it was their own fault like Dad said.

The doubt plagued me. It felt like a sickness seeping into my veins, hardening them, and slowly killing me. I didn't like it. I didn't *want* it.

"Do it," Dad said. "Prove to me you're still Pure, Junior, or you'll be the one on the table next."

Slowly, I took the knife from his hand. Winnie shook her head, back and forth, back and forth, faster and faster.

There was a scream. And blood, so much blood.

There's a bush in front of Winnie's house. It's dead; all the red roses are dried up from being neglected. Long stemmed roses were my mother's favorite. I wonder what my mother's crime was? Why did she have to die? What made her a Corrupt?

"Corwin!"

I forced myself to look up to the building. Winnie was hanging out one of the windows, waving at me. If she was a Corrupt, if all the others in her house were too, then I had decided I would rather be Corrupt than Pure.

Two weeks ago, I stabbed my father to save another. We ran out and haven't seen him since. I didn't want to kill him, just maim him, so we could get away, but if he were alive … I think we'd have seen him by now.

What I did was impure. Wrong, so wrong. There was a disgusting feeling of gooey guilt clogging up my heart, making it hard to go on, but every day with Winnie, every smile of hers, life got a little easier.

TIME TO PRAY

E.B. Black

I'VE NEVER BEEN RELIGIOUS, but I take the time to pray every day. A feeling of dread, like a shadow, overcomes me. I close my eyes, bow my head, and beg God to protect my body and soul.

When I open my eyes again, things in my house always look different. Sometimes the furniture has rearranged itself or the knife I was slicing onions with is pointed at me instead of away. Sometimes windows are open that had been closed and doors have slammed themselves shut.

I own no pets and have no room mates. I wish I could blame it on someone else or claim it was some kind of prank being played on me. But as long as I remember to pray, I know I will always be safe.

I've had an ad running in the newspaper for a while, asking for a roommate. Few people apply and most people are jumpy when I interview them. I've called them back, begging them to move in. But none of them even answer the phone. It seems they take one look at me and my house and never want to come back. I wish I knew what was bothering them.

I hear the little kids of the neighborhood shouting in front of my place. They think I can't hear them or the ghostly way they groan at one another. They dare each other to ring the doorbell and see if "the crazy lady" answers. Sometimes I'm tempted to open my window and shout obscenities at them. A horror show they expect, a horror show they'll get, but I don't because I don't want to make it worse.

The truth is, part of me is afraid they are right. I don't remember moving the furniture, I'm not even strong enough to do so, but who else could be doing it?

My house has been egged and spray painted. People have broken the windows. I wish I could move, but I can't afford the mortgage payments anywhere else.

As long as I close my eyes and pray whenever the feeling of dread floods through me, I'm always okay. It makes me uneasy, but as long as I continue to do what has worked in the past, there's nothing to be afraid of.

I am baking cookies when the doorbell rings. It seems the kids have finally worked up the bravery to bother me.

I consider ignoring them. This can't lead anywhere good, but the doorbell rings again, so I sigh and answer the call.

A little boy with the biggest brown eyes I've ever seen smiles at me and says hello.

I cross my arms. "Can I help you?"

"I'm your next door neighbor, Mike. I'm nine years old and just moved here. The other little kids keep talking about how this place is haunted, but I know that's not true and want to prove it to all of them by coming inside."

"Where's your mother?"

Mike shrugs. "She thinks I'm at my friend's house. I need to prove the truth to her as well. She banned me from coming here."

I'm tempted to say no—his mother disapproves—but why should I have to tolerate being treated that way? Why are parents trying to protect their kids from me? Maybe if Mike and I become friends, everyone will change their mind.

"I'm Jezebel." I move out of the way. "Come in."

Mike takes off his blue baseball cap and fiddles with it as he enters my home.

I take the cookies out of the oven. "You're the first visitor I've had since I moved here and I can't tell you how thankful I am that someone is bothering to talk to me."

Mike laughs. "Don't mind everyone else. Most of them are just little kids. They'll learn the truth when they are older." He says all this in the sweetest, little voice imaginable.

I pull a spatula out of a drawer and start putting the cookies on a plate to cool. "Would you like one?"

Mike sniffs the air. "They smell delicious. I'll take two, please, ma'am."

I put two cookies on a plate and pour him a glass of milk. He struggles to climb on a stool near my counter top. I sit across from him with my own plate of cookies.

Mike talks while we eat. "I know you're not a ghost because there's no such thing as ghosts. I used to get afraid that there was a monster in my closet when I went to sleep, then one day I faced it and realized it was only a shadow. I've never been afraid of monsters and ghosts since. There's always an explanation for everything."

I smile. "You're pretty wise for someone so young."

Mike shrugs. "That's what my mom always tells me."

I laugh. "Of course she does."

As we eat, the feeling of dread overwhelms me. A shadow crosses over my eyes and I can feel it coming. It's time to pray.

This has never happened when someone else was in the house. I'm not sure what to do.

I grab Mike's hand. "Do you ever pray?" The shadow is closer. It's so near that I can almost touch it. I need to hurry.

Mike shakes his head. "No, ma'am. My mom takes me to church, but I think there must be other explanations for God, too."

My heart thuds in my chest. I begin to panic. "This one time, can you pray with me?"

"I don't know-" He tilts his head and lets go of my hand.

I close my eyes. I can't wait anymore. I hope he listens to my request, but there's nothing more I can do to convince him now. The shadow is right in front of me.

Dear God, please save my soul. Protect my body and my heart from the threats that loom nearby. Don't let me be devoured. Save me from the hunger.

The feeling of dread disappears. I should have prayed for Mike as well, just in case, but there isn't time now.

I open my eyes. Nothing has changed. The cookies are still on our plates, one of Mike's half eaten. The glasses haven't been knocked over. None of the furniture has moved. There's only one big difference, Mike is gone.

"Mike!" I shout. My breathing grows rapid. I search around the counter, but Mike is nowhere to be found.

Did I hurt him? Did someone else hurt him? Is he hiding?

"Mike," I shout. "Please come out. This isn't funny. Your mother will be worried."

But all I am greeted with is silence. I really should play music in my house.

I notice a spot of blood on the floor. I walk up to it and discover a tiny trail of blood that leads down the hallway and to my bedroom.

I push open the door, wincing and terrified of what I will find.

"Mike," I call out, hoping desperately he will respond. At this point, I assume he must be hurt and I'll need to call 9-1-1, but still there's no response.

I notice his blue baseball cap on my bed and approach it slowly, timidly. It's stained red with blood. I touch it. It's still wet and warm. Bile rises in my throat and my stomach turns.

"Mike, please." I collapse to my knees next to the bed, sure that Mike is not going to answer. Tears pour down my face. How could this happen? Mike was the first person in this neighborhood to be nice to me.

The evil I pray against had never hurt anyone before. It scared me, but the worst it did was rearrange things. What if the evil thing is me? If it is, then I just killed Mike! And if it's not, what have I been living with this whole time? Now that this thing has had a taste of blood, will it come for me next?

I realize I can't call the police. They're going to assume I did it and send me to jail. Who would ever buy the story that I just closed my eyes and there was suddenly blood everywhere? It's the worst defense ever.

A loud knock on my front door causes me to jump to my feet. My heart is pounding so hard. I can't answer the door. But the doorbell rings again.

I thought I hated being left alone all the time, but this is worse. I have to figure out what to do about Mike quickly.

Shouting filters through the door. "Open up! I know my son Mike is in there! If you don't open this door, I'll call the police!"

I rush over, wiping away my tears and straightening up my clothes. What can I do to make her go away?

I barely open the door and peek my head outside. I put on a stern face to hide my panic.

His mother's hair is in rollers. Her eyes are wide open and her robe is loose. "Let me in, right now!"

Poor woman—if only she knew it was too late. I can't let her in; she'll see the truth.

The woman glances over my shoulder. Holding the door shut to keep her from getting inside, I glance, too. The countertop bar where Mike and I had been eating hides Mike's blood from her view.

Mike's mother pushes against the door. "Open the door already. Mike loves cookies. You wouldn't have set two places for yourself."

I push back. "Leave me alone. I've never seen your kid before!"

"Stop lying! The neighbors all saw him come in here. I know Mike was here."

I struggle to slam the door in her face and finally succeed. As I am struggling to lock it, too, a shadow passes by me. I feel the dread flooding through me.

Not now. This can't be happening now. It never happens more than once a day. I usually get a day or two break.

Why is it so hard to lock the door? I have to do it now or Mike's Mother might come in and something bad could happen to her, too.

I struggle and hear a click as I close my eyes. I hope I succeeded, but I no longer have the luxury of checking. I begin to pray.

Please, God. Don't let me be devoured. Protect me from evil. Save my soul and my flesh. I need to be rescued.

I know the prayers are important for many reasons. Whatever this shadow is, not only am I not allowed to see it, I don't think I'm really supposed to hear it either. The chants in my head are there to distract me from the noise.

I feel relief and open my eyes again. I had weakened my hold on the door while I was praying and Mike's mother bursts through the doorway and shoves me aside. I guess I hadn't locked it after all.

There's nothing I can do now. I must accept whatever my fate may be. I can always try telling Mike's mom the truth. Maybe she'll believe me. But one look into her wide, shifty blue eyes and I know that she'll never buy any story.

I follow her as she walks over to the countertop.

The cookies are all gone. Even the ones that had still been cooling. There's not a crumb or a pan to be seen anywhere.

Mike's mother gestures wildly at my kitchen. "But I saw the plate of food here just a minute ago."

So that's what was changed this time around. That was pretty convenient.

But there was more. The trail of blood that led to my bedroom was gone and Mike's hat had also disappeared. Mike's mother wandered frantically from room to room, opening closets and doors and shouting Mike's name.

I cross my arms, a smirk on my face as she winds down and gives up.

I open the door and gesture for her to go outside. "Are you done harassing me now?"

Her face turns red and she points her finger at me. "I know he was here and I will find out the truth."

I all but push her outside as she continues to threaten me. I slam the door in her face and lock it. This time, I double-check the lock. She can yell at my closed door all she wants.

But as silence settles over me, fear clutches my heart. I shouldn't have wanted to be alone again. I should ask for Mike's mother to come back. As scary as she and the police are, they aren't as frightening to me as whatever killed Mike. At least I can see them, hear them, touch them, predict them. Maybe spending a night in jail would be better than spending another night here.

Tears form in my eyes. Poor Mike, punished for being kind-hearted and believing the best in people.

I won't let him just die. I will do something about it. Next time I have to pray, I will open my eyes and face whatever it is. Maybe I'll be able to find Mike or at least his body. It's the least I can do for his mom.

I swallow loudly, my heart full of dread.

Three days pass without an incident.

Then, one day, after I finished watering my garden and re-entered my home, the feeling of dread came.

It took me so off guard that I had to lean against a pillar in order to keep myself from fainting.

It's time to pray. I need to pray. I can't do this. I can't handle seeing this thing. I start to close my eyes, but I shake my head and reopen them.

I have to fight for Mike. It's selfish if I close my eyes now.

The feeling of dread increases. There's so much pressure. I'm trembling all over. My eyes are so wide now they feel dry. My knees feel too weak to keep me upright.

My brain shouts at me to stop—that this will be the biggest mistake of my life. But I can't let someone else get hurt. I need to find out what is going on.

Then blindness.

At first I thought I gave in and prayed, but I blink as I listen to the steady beep of the hospital sounds around me. I believe my eyes are open, but I see nothing.

The nurses don't know I am awake. I can hear them gossiping to each other as they fiddle with equipment around me.

The first nurse speaks. "They say that she was attacked. That someone must have broken into her house and ripped her eyeballs out."

The second nurse sounds sad. "The poor woman."

"The weird thing is, they looked for broken locks or glass and there was no sign of a break-in. If someone did get inside, they must have been living there already or had their own key."

I know what the people in my neighborhood will say when they find out. They'll say that I did this to myself. I was a crazy woman, who scared their kids, and made that boy, Mike, disappear. They'll say I was suicidal or couldn't live with myself and what I'd done.

Once I'm able, I'll talk to therapists who will question me about what happened, I'll tell them I have no memory of it. I'll spend the rest of my life struggling to know how to explain my blindness to others to escape their judgment.

I would cling to the story that a homeless man was living in my house and I heard him walking around a few times. I'd even make up imaginary stories about the few times I spotted him either using the toilet or stealing my food.

But deep down inside, I know that isn't the truth. Whenever I start to remember, a feeling of dread overcomes me and I start to pray.

I start to recall what it felt like to dig my nails into my eyeballs. I remember their squish and the juice and how it felt to rip through them like they were nothing. It's amazing the strength your hands have when adrenaline is coursing through your veins—you can pull apart anything; you don't feel any pain while you're harming yourself.

Because the truth is, after I'd seen what had killed Mike, I didn't want to see anymore. I ripped my own eyes out. It is easier to pretend that someone else did it to me.

Once I delude myself about that, I might force myself to forget the face I saw when I opened my eyes that one time I was supposed to pray. I know that if I remember what it looked like I'd lose the last bit of sanity I had left.

My blindness assures me I'll never be forced to see that face again.

But whenever the memory returns and the dread overwhelms me, I bow my head and pray.

My prayers are always answered.

LOST SOLES

Madeline Mora-Summonte

THE LOWRY SISTERS WEREN'T supposed to be at the beach that night.

The family was due to leave for home the next morning, another vacation over and done. The girls begged to check on the sea turtle nest one more time. The eggs were supposed to hatch soon. But their mother had already rinsed bathing suits, and their father had already set the alarm clock for an early start to beat the traffic.

The girls crept out—Sammi in pink slippers, Audrey in yellow sneakers, both wearing pajamas. They left behind rumpled covers and treasured teddy bears. They'd be back soon.

Dark clouds, heavy with rain, gathered overhead and watched the two small shadows skitter down the deserted road, hurry through the isolated parking lot.

That night, the hatchlings made their way to the sea, made their way home.

They were the only children who did.

Harley gently moves a mildewed teddy bear out of the way so she can lock her bike onto the bench's leg. The memorial to the Lowry sisters is disintegrating, its pieces scattering to wherever grief goes when time says it must move on. She tugs on the lock, which is worth more than her old clunker of a bike. But she's not taking any chances. Ray gave her the bike many years ago, when they first moved to the beach. She refuses to lose the bike to hooligans. If she could've locked up her husband, kept cancer—the biggest hooligan of all—from stealing him, she would've done it.

She tucks her sandals into the bike's basket then heads down to where the sea slaps the shore. The water surrounds her ankles—warm, caressing—until it pulls at her, insistent, a cranky child wanting attention. She turns left and starts walking, her movements automatic. As usual, the beach is mostly empty, and Harley's gaze wanders, searches for hope.

She knows it's silly. Too much time has gone by for the beach to offer up any clues about what happened to those little girls. The Lowry sisters' Missing Poster stays folded in her pocket, soft now, creased, like her own face, like the girls' faces will never be. Those girls were taken, either by the sea or by strangers. Not everything can be locked up. Things, people, are taken all the time. Harley knows she's not going to find those girls. What she wants to find are answers.

Harley plods along. Sandpipers, their feathers rustling in the breeze, hustle past as if she's in their way. Her body is thin yet heavy with age and grief. She's all knees and elbows again, like she was as a child, only without all of the energy and joy. More than ever, she's aware of how her body is both hers and not hers, how she really is only renting it. It'll be time to return it soon.

At the jetty, she rests, watches a brown pelican skim the water then dive for breakfast. Harley squints. Something yellow bobs near the rocks. She shifts to get a better angle, but she still can't see. As if with a sly wink, the sea slides it closer. Its shape snags Harley's heart. She clambers over the jetty. Small waves, smacking against the rocks like wet kisses, push the object into a crevice. It waits, for her.

A small, yellow sneaker.

Harley sprawls, laying down her bones, her sharp edges grinding against the rocks' sharp edges beneath her. She stretches. Reaches. As her fingers catch the slimy white laces, something splashes into the water nearby. She doesn't turn, doesn't look. She pulls the sneaker to her, rolls on her side, and sits up.

She doesn't pull out the Missing Poster. She's looked at the photo too often, too long. This sneaker belongs to Audrey Lowry. In Harley's hands is the closest thing to an answer anyone has. The girls didn't disappear without a trace. They most likely made it to the beach, most likely were taken by the sea.

The police. Harley reaches inside her right pocket for her phone, frowns. Pats her left pocket. Nothing. It's then she remembers the small splash. Taking a quick look around, she spots her phone submerged in a pool of water. She pulls it out, half-heartedly pushes the buttons. It's dead.

She jams it into her pocket, considers her next step. If she doesn't run into anyone with a phone, she'll ride her bike to the picnic grounds, use the pay phone by the restrooms. She picks her way off the rocks. Breaking a hip now is not going to do anyone any good.

Gray clouds smudge the sky. The wind whips by as if on its way to somewhere important. Harley doesn't see another soul as she hurries back across the beach.

She's out of breath by the time she spots the bench where she locked up her bike. She hurries up the sand, only to stop, stunned. "No." The word, wrecked, shredded, like the pieces of the Lowry sisters' memorial.

Her bike is gone.

"No." Louder now, with a stamp of her foot like a little girl throwing a tantrum, a little girl mad at the unfairness of life, a little girl upset she can't go to the sea turtle nest one more time.

The sneaker falls to the sand as Harley kicks the bench, rattles the broken lock left behind. Today of all days hooligans steal her beloved bike. She takes a big, shuddery breath, decides she'll be pissed off and sad later. Right now, she has more important things to do, like get to that pay phone.

The clouds furrow like a scowling brow. The sea churns, turbulent, nauseating. Harley picks up the sneaker. The white sole is marred by blue streaks, like dripped paint. Letters, words, printed by a child's hand, are smeared beyond recognition. Almost.

Help. White. Truck.

The sea did not take the Lowry sisters.

Harley gasps, the sound small, vulnerable on the deserted beach. She looks around, notices for the first time how truly alone she is. Fear tries to take hold but she won't let it. She can't. She has no idea how that sneaker ended up in the sea, has no idea how Audrey Lowry managed to write a message on it, but those girls could still be out there somewhere, could still be alive.

Harley hurries through the wooded area and over the small bridge toward the picnic grounds. Her bare feet land hard on burrs, on broken shells but she feels nothing until she catches one funny. It slices into the bottom of her foot.

"Ow!" She stops. The cut is deep, ragged. The nearby bushes shiver, rustle. Harley jerks her head around. Above her, the wind gets the palm fronds whispering, sets the Spanish moss swaying.

"The wind," she confirms, even as an icy finger of dread traces its way up her spine. A lump forms in her throat but she swallows it down. Now is not the time to act like a frightened old lady.

As she continues on, she feels eyes on her. Every step brings a quiet whimper of pain and fear. She limps along as fast as she can, leaving a blood trail behind.

She allows herself one strangled sob when she spots the phone hanging on the wall between the men's and ladies' rooms. She clutches the yellow sneaker with one hand, pulls herself up the rickety stairs with the other.

Thunder shakes the sky. She cowers beneath the overhang and grabs the receiver off the hook. The broken cord whips at her. She recoils as if it's a snake. Rage and terror rise in her, and she hurls the receiver as far away as she can. Lightning sizzles its support.

Harley stumbles into the ladies' room, into a stall. She sinks down onto the closed toilet. She rests the sneaker in her lap, stares at her bloody prints on the worn linoleum. Her foot hurts, and she's more scared than she's ever been, scared of something she refuses to find the words for. But she has to keep walking. She has to.

Outside, heavy footsteps shudder the old building. She stills. Raindrops splatter the roof. The ladies' room door creaks open.

As quietly as she can, Harley locks the stall.

On the other side, big, dirty, work boots turn toward her. The lock jiggles.

She traces Audrey Lowry's useless plea for help over and over with trembling fingers.

The other yellow sneaker falls to the floor. It lands with a small thump in one of the bloody footprints Harley left behind.

THE TROLLS

Kay Elam

SOME PEOPLE SAY I'M SUPERSTITIOUS, but I know I ain't. I got good reasons for what I believe. And my reasons ain't nobody's business but my own. I don't step on cracks in sidewalks. But it ain't 'cause I'm afraid I'll break my mama's back (or nobody else's for that matter). One time I tripped on a stupid crack and skinned my knee...that's all. And I always sit with my back to a corner when I'm in a restaurant. It ain't 'cause I'm afraid some terrorists or something's gonna get me but 'cause I get cold real easy like, and it's always warmer sitting in a corner. And, I don't even think throwing salt over my shoulder *is* a superstition; it's more like a habit, you know, like putting catsup on your french fries. You just do it 'cause everybody else in your family does it, and you grew up doing it and don't know no different. By the time you see everybody else don't do it that way, it's done become a habit, and habits are hard to break. Everybody knows that. Just ask anybody who smokes, which I *don't*, 'cept when nobody's looking.

So, I ain't superstitious at all…I got good reasons for what I do.

My story starts several weeks ago when I found out my shift at the plant was gonna change from seven to three to three to eleven. Later on that day, I got called in by the HR lady. Now I'm a good worker, but I was afraid I was gonna get a pink slip anyways. They'd been handing 'em out like candy for over a week.

"Jessica," she said, "I have a favor to ask."

Hum, I thought. *That don't sound like she's firing me…least not today.* "Yes ma'am?" I always mind my manners when talking to management.

"We've got two employees who live near you in Grady who've also been changed to second shift."

"Yes ma'am."

"Before, they rode over with a senior worker who is staying on first."

I could see where this was going, and I didn't like it none. "Uh huh."

"Do you think it would be possible for you to give them a ride to and from work every day? They'd help with your expenses, of course."

I stood there like a bump on a log trying to think of some reason to say "no way in hell," but couldn't come up with a single thing with her looking at me over them there purple half-rimmed glasses covered in rhinestones.

She musta seen I weren't fond of the idea 'cause she kept on talking. "The company would appreciate it, and I'd consider it a personal favor."

Now, you don't have to hit me over the head with a two-by-four for me to get her meaning. She did the schedule and decided who worked what shift. If I didn't do it, I'd be on nights forever. But if I did, maybe I could go back to days the next time they redid the schedule.

"'Course, Miz Brown. I'd be happy to have the company," I lied.

She clapped her hands. "I knew you'd say yes. I told them to meet you at the table by the Pepsi machine in the lunchroom during the second break today. Their names are Walter Reynolds and Sandra Martin. Walter works in the tooling department, and Sandra's clerical. I'd hate to lose either of them because of transportation issues."

"Yes ma'am," I said as I left her dingy second floor office.

Maybe it wouldn't be too bad I tried to tell myself. At least I won't be driving Route 32 all by myself in the middle of the night.

Route 32 had to be the curviest road in the county. It musta been laid out by some drunk guy on drugs. The road's so narrow I can barely keep my eight-year-old Honda 'tween the double yellow lines in the middle and the white line on the edge as I zig-zag 'round the curves. I hardly ever go over thirty-five. When there *is* a straight stretch, hills pop up like sand dunes at the beach.

Truth be told, I ain't never been to no beach, but I know sand dunes are a lot bigger than ant hills, and I am an expert on them. I tumbled into a fire ant bed when I was little, and before I knew what hit me, my Granny'd done rubbed me down in kerosene. Scared me pert near to death. I was afraid she was gonna light a match and burn me up. But she was just trying to kill the ants crawling up and down my arms and legs. Then she sent me out back for a head-to-toe scrubbing with lye soap in the wash tub while she poured the rest of the kerosene on the ant bed itself. I think, but I ain't sure, she set *it* on fire. I didn't go anywhere near that part of the yard for months.

Anyhow, the best thing I can say about that road is I pretty much have it to myself. Most everybody else, including the cops, takes the new interstate a few miles over. That to say, the road ain't only curvy, it's hilly too.

I don't drive on interstates, or even four-lane highways if I can help it. Not since I was in the eleventh grade and involved in a wreck so bad it shut the road down for over a day. The wreck weren't my fault, and I weren't hurt none, praise the Lord, but when I opened my car door to get out, Timmy Reynolds's head rolled right by my feet. He was in my class at school. I screamed, jumped back in my car, and locked the doors. I had nightmares about cut-off heads and car wrecks for years.

Anyhow, when I walked in the lunchroom, I spotted my future tag-alongs. It looked like they already knew each other 'cause they was deep in conversation. I hung back and watched. The guy looked older than my twenty-two years and was tall and gangly. He had dark stringy hair that needed a cut. The girl was a little bitty thang, prob'ly no more than nineteen, maybe twenty, and had eyes so blue I could see 'em across the room. Her curly blond hair bounced when she talked, just like the rest of her. I kept my mousy brown hair pulled up in a ponytail so it wouldn't look like a mop head. I ain't fat for being 5'6," but I felt like a hog next to her.

The guy spotted me so I walked on over.

"Hey," I said. "I'm Jessie. The HR lady said y'all needed a ride for second shift."

They looked at each other. The guy spoke. "I'm Walter and this is Sandra." He tilted his head toward the girl 'fore he turned back to me. "You're Bud Mitchell's kid sister, aren't you?"

I was caught off guard. "Yep. Don't remind me." I smiled, but I didn't mean it.

He grinned. "Thought I recognized you."

"How'd you know Bud?" I asked.

"Army. We were in the Middle East together. He showed me a picture of you once. Said the two of you were real close. What's he doing these days?"

"Last I heard, he was seeing the country. Been gone a while."

"Well, when you hear from him again, tell him Walter says hey."

"Will do," I said. "You guys interested in a ride or not? Break's almost over."

"What kind of car you got?" he asked.

"Honda Accord. That matter?"

"No. Just asking." He looked at the girl again then back at me. "We'll fill your tank once a week in exchange for a ride back and forth to work every day. That sound fair?

Did that sound fair? I could go two weeks on a tank of gas, even with the commute to work, sometimes longer.

"Um…why don't you each pay me $20 a week? A tank of gas is more than $40 so that's a good deal for y'all."

Walter and Sandra turned their backs to me and whispered. I strained to hear, but couldn't.

"That works," Walter said. "New schedule starts Monday. We'll meet you at the Exxon by the interstate at 2:15."

I coughed. "Um…I don't drive on the interstate. I come route 32."

"Ewww," Sandra piped in. "I don't want to come on that old road. It's spooky."

Walter looked back and forth between us, like he was trying to make a decision. Finally he said, "OK, but you gotta pick us up at our houses."

"Where do you live?" Maybe this was gonna be my way outta taking on passengers. If it were too far outta my way, I'd just tell the HR lady I couldn't pick 'em up and get to work on time.

But, they lived pretty close to each other, and I passed right by their streets on my way in. I didn't have no excuse. "I'll pick you up by two. Be ready, 'cause if you ain't, I'm coming without you. I ain't gonna be late 'cause I'm waiting on you."

When Sandra started to whine, first about the time, then again about the route, Walter shushed her. He said he'd protect her. Who was he, Superman? Didn't matter, he shut her up, but he creeped me out. There was something about him…

We started our routine the next week, and it was all right for a while. Walter sat up front 'cause he had such long legs. Sandra leaned forward between us even though I told her to put her seatbelt on.

For the most part, I didn't talk much in the car. Sandra rattled on, but I tuned her out. When she asked a question I didn't want to answer, I'd turn the radio on. Walter wasn't as easy to ignore.

We'd been carpooling, if you can call it that since I had the only car, for about six weeks when Walter asked the question I'd been a dreading. "Why don't you use the interstate?"

"None of your business…and I don't want to talk about it." I reached forward and turned on the radio.

He turned it off. "You were in the big wreck six years ago, weren't you?"

I opened and closed my mouth, but nothing came out.

"What wreck?" Sandra asked. Something always came out of her mouth, usually drivel. "I didn't live here six years ago. What wreck?"

Walter cleared his throat. "I was away in the army, but from what I understand, it was an icy morning. Traffic was creeping along down the steep hill on the four-lane that runs by the river. Near the curve at the bottom, it'd pretty much come to a stop. A tractor-trailer truck lost its brakes and plowed over several cars. It didn't stop until it hit another eighteen-wheeler and jackknifed. Both trucks caught on fire. I don't know how many people were killed. I'm not sure they ever got a final body count. It was rush hour. I heard some bodies were destroyed so bad they were never found. Cars couldn't even be identified. Is that about it?" he asked me.

I nodded. The knot in my throat felt big as a gourd, and I couldn't say a word. Tears ran down my cheeks. Why'd he have to give a play by play? I'd been in an outside lane, and my car had been shoved into a ditch out of the way.

"And you were in the wreck?" Walter asked.

I nodded.

"Hurt?"

I shook my head.

"Need me to drive now?"

I shook my head again. Nobody drove my car but me. "I'm OK," I said, wiping my eyes on my sleeve.

"My brother was killed in that wreck," he said. He was all calm-like, like he was giving the weather.

"Oh my God, you're Timmy's brother?"

He nodded.

I started shaking like a leaf. I pulled to the side of the road. I felt like I might puke.

Sandra patted my shoulder and handed me a napkin so I could blow my nose.

Walter just sat there with his arms crossed looking at his watch. "If we don't get going, we're gonna be late."

A couple of weeks later on our way to work, we saw a portajohn sitting about twenty-five feet off the road near some picnic tables by the river that ran through town.

"Where'd that come from?" I asked.

"I don't know," Sandra said, "but I'm glad to see it. Sometimes I have to tinkle on the way home, and there's no place to stop."

"I'll stop anywhere you want," I told her. "I'll even put a roll of toilet paper in the back, but I ain't gonna stop at no portajohn."

"Why not?" Walter asked. "Did you almost fall in one as a kid?"

"No. I thank they're nasty, and I don't want their germs all over my car."

"Oh, there's a story here," Sandra said. "I can tell, there's a story. What's the story?"

I turned up the radio and sang along until she started talking about something else.

But she was oh so right. There was a story…

Every time we passed the portajohn, Sandra asked to stop, and every time, I said no. I knew she didn't have to pee. She was just ribbing me. I got in the habit of speeding on that stretch of road. It weren't like there was ever a cop out there to give me a ticket.

But she wouldn't stop. Finally, to shut her up (and maybe scare her just a little bit), I told her I'd tell her why I wouldn't stop on the way home that night.

As soon as we got in the car, she said, "You didn't forget, did you? You promised."

"I didn't forget."

"I brought hot chocolate," she said.

That was actually kind of sweet. Whether I liked it or not, she was growing on me. I drank my hot chocolate and took a deep breath.

I told her that when I'd been a little girl, my mama took my brother and me to visit our granny every summer. During one stretch of the drive, there were outhouses next to every farm house we passed. But these weren't just any toilets. They looked like the houses they sat by, right down to the windows and curtains. I thought they were beautiful. Every year I begged for one for Christmas. 'Course we had indoor plumbing and didn't need one for *that*, but I'd planned to turn it into a playhouse for me and my dolls.

That's when my mama told me to stop pestering her. She said I didn't want one of them for a playhouse because trolls lived in 'em. I told her trolls lived under bridges, but she said these were special trolls that fed on people, especially little girls who asked lots of questions. She said the farmers who had the outhouses kept the trolls locked up during the day and let 'em out to feed at night. The only way to protect yourself against 'em was to put lamb's blood or wool on your door.

She scared the bejesus out of me. I started crying, and when we got to Granny's, I begged Mama to sleep with me. She had nothing to do with that 'cause after putting me to bed, she went out juke-jointing with her high school friends. 'Course I didn't know nothing about that at the time. I just knew I was afraid to go to sleep. And I didn't have any lamb's blood or wool, so before I went to bed, I stuck my finger with a sewing needle, put a few drops on the door, and prayed it'd work.

I didn't tell my riders my big brother slept with me so I wouldn't be scared. I didn't tell 'em that was when he started molesting me either. No one knew about that but me…and him…and God, I guess.

All three of us laughed at my silly story.

"I know it was make believe," I said, "and I know portajohns are different from outhouses, but both give me the creeps. That's why I don't want to stop. So, that there's your story."

* * * * *

The Friday before Halloween, the company had one of its morale-building dinners. Some of the food must've gone bad 'cause we weren't five miles from the factory before all three of our stomachs were singing out of tune. I was having trouble focusing on the road. Walter was throwing up in a McDonald's bag that'd been in the floorboard. When we got close to the portajohn, Sandra insisted on stopping.

"I'll stop somewhere else, and you can go behind some bushes," I told her.

"Look, missy," she said. "If you don't want shit all over the back seat of your car, I strongly suggest you get to that john as fast as you can."

I felt too bad to argue. I pulled in with the headlights shining right on the door. There was a huge padlock. No way she was getting in there. *Thank you Jesus.*

"I've got to get in," she whined.

Walter pulled his head from the McDonald's bag and looked out the window. "I can pick that lock in no time. Fresh air will do me good."

Great, I thought. I could probably use some fresh air too, but no way I was leaving the car. I'd just roll my window down. And I'd for sure keep the car running and the doors locked.

Turned out Walter couldn't pick the lock, so he broke it with a crowbar from my trunk. That lock was useless. I wondered why they put a portajohn there anyways if they was gonna keep it locked…unless it was only locked at night… Sandra did her business while Walter puked in the bushes near the river.

Finally, we made it home. Before I went upstairs to bed, sick as I was, I defrosted some lamb chops in the microwave and, feeling like a fool, smeared the blood on my front door. For good measure, I used duct tape to tape the chops underneath the wreath hanging up there.

* * * * *

The next day, Saturday, was Halloween. I woke up feeling like I had a hangover. I would've loved to have pulled the covers over my head and stayed in bed, but I had errands to run and because of the night before, my list had grown.

I picked up the candy for the trick-or-treaters. That was easy. But now I had to figure out how to keep the trolls out without seeming like a nut. At least it was Halloween.

I went to the fabric store and bought a lamb's wool blanket more or less the size of my front door. Then, I went 'cross-town to a butcher and asked for a gallon of lamb's blood. No way I was going to the butcher near my house. He knew me. The big, burly man rolled his eyes, mumbled something about witches, and came back with a gallon jug of dark red liquid.

My plan was to soak the blanket in the blood. I just had to figure out how to keep it from stinking to high heaven. I went to a store that sold expensive little bottles of what they called *therapeutic essence oils.* I couldn't outright ask what would mix well with lamb's blood so I told 'em I had a sick mama who had open bedsores that bled a lot and asked their advice on getting rid of the odor. They told me I needed *aromatherapy* and had ideas about oils my imaginary sick mama could breathe in to maybe prevent the sores. So, of course, I bought everything they suggested, including a *misting diffuser* to go beside her imaginary bed. Hum…I might enjoy the smells, though. They said they was relaxing, and boy could I use some relaxing.

When I got home I put the blanket in the guest bathtub. I weren't about to put it in *my* tub. I took baths in that thing! I mixed the oil with the blood before dying the blanket. I wrung it as much as I could, then hung it over the shower rod to dry. Couldn't hang it on the door 'til it was dry 'cause the blood'd drip on the porch. It turned out pretty good, if I do say so myself.

I went back out and got a scarecrow. I found a lamb's wool sweater in the children's department at Walmart I could dress it in. After Thanksgiving, I'd put up a snowman and use the sweater on it too, then after that, well…I'd cross that bridge when I come to it.

I thought about calling Walter and Sandra to see how they was feeling, but we weren't friends, and I didn't want 'em to get the wrong idea. I'd find out Monday afternoon.

I stopped by Walter's first. He was pale, said he felt like he'd had the stomach flu all weekend, but was better now.

When we got to Sandra's street, blue lights flashed like a convention of Kmart specials. *What was going on?* We edged up to her house, which was covered in that yellow crime tape.

"What's happening?" I asked the first policeman I saw. "We're here to pick up Sandra Martin. She rides to work with us."

"When's the last time you saw Ms. Martin?" the officer asked, motioning a detective over.

"Friday night, a little after midnight," I said. "We'd all ate something at work that made us sick so we got home a little later than usual, but not that much. We dropped her off first and watched her go in the house."

The detective and Sandra's mom walked over to us. Her mom looked like she'd been crying for days.

"I heard her come in Friday night," her mom said, but I didn't get up. "I could just kick myself, but she comes in every night around midnight. I don't go to sleep until I hear her, but I don't get up. The next morning she was gone. Her bed hadn't even been slept in."

The detective wrote something down. "Mrs. Martin called in a missing person's report Saturday morning, but we don't usually start looking for an adult for twenty-four to forty-eight hours. Nine times out of ten, they show up on their own."

"I couldn't remember who she was riding to work with now, and the plant was shut down all weekend," her mom said. "I tried to call you, Walter, but didn't get an answer."

"Um, my ringer must have been turned off." He looked down and shuffled his feet. "I was sick all weekend and stayed home and slept."

"Nothing seems amiss in her room," the detective said. "Are you sure she went into the house? Maybe she went in and then left with someone else."

"I'm sure," I said. "My mama'd have my hide if I dropped somebody off and didn't watch to make sure she got inside safe. I was raised right. Besides we was all sick as dogs, probably food poisoning. She had some serious diarrhea. She was headed straight to the bathroom."

Walter nodded but his eyes were staring off in the distance. I knew he had a thing for that little airhead.

The detective got our names and numbers and told us he'd be in touch.

As we headed to work, I made a stop at a hardware store and bought a lock.

"What's that for?" Walter asked.

"It's for you to put on that outhouse when we drive by it on our way to work."

"You can't be serious."

"As a heart attack."

He looked at me the same way he used to look at Sandra… the same way my brother used to look at me…until he looked at me one time too many.

It was three years ago, right after Bud was discharged from the army. Mama had gone off with her latest boyfriend. I don't even remember his name.

My brother had started messing with me again. I asked him if he'd take me to see the outhouses I'd loved so much as a little girl. He was happy to oblige.

We went at night. There're been a full moon, but it'd played peek-a-boo behind the clouds. All the way there, we'd laughed about how much the troll story had frightened me as a little girl and how he'd slept with me to *protect* me.

All the houses with matching outhouses that had once seemed so beautiful were now empty. I picked one to stop at, and we parked behind the big house.

I suggested we get out and look around, although I'd already been there a few days earlier. I knew what was in the deserted house, the barn, and the outhouse. I knew it by heart.

We were in the house when he said he thought he saw a troll. I laughed. Any trolls that had ever been there were long gone, just like the people. I weren't afraid of them. 'Course I didn't tell him that.

"I think you need protecting," he said.

"You can't see a troll in here," I said. "They'd be by the outhouse." With that I giggled and ran out the door toward the outhouse.

He chased me, like I knew he would, playing hide and seek along the way.

"Will you check, just in case?" I asked sweetly, a little flirty.

He sighed, but did as I asked. "Ain't nothing in here but me. Come on in and see for yourself." When I walked in, he grabbed me, like I knew he would, and started tearing off my clothes.

The outhouse was bigger than most. It was a two-holer.

"Hang on," I said. "Just in case, will you look down the holes…please?"

He laughed. "For you, sis, anything."

When he bent to look down the seat of the shitter, I raised the axe I'd left in the corner and clobbered him over the head.

It knocked him out. I went to the car and got out a tarp I'd put in the trunk. I lugged it inside and rolled him onto it before I chopped off his head. I'd already seen one severed head. What's two? I wrapped it in plastic so it wouldn't drip and dropped it down the hole. *Plump.*

I chopped off his arms and legs careful to keep all the blood on the tarp. I liked the sound the blade of the axe made as it sliced through bone. I figured he'd rot in all the shit in the hole, but just in case, I poured a big bag of lye I'd put in my trunk down the hole to eat up his bones. I spread another bag on his torso, which was still on the tarp. It was a struggle, but I managed to wrap him up and cram his body down the hole. Good thing he was skinny. I dropped the axe on top. I wiped my hands together and told myself I'd done a good job. I'd never have to worry about that troll again.

When Mama got home a few days later I told her he'd decided to hike across the country—like she cared.

"On second thought," I told Walter, "we're gonna be late for work if we put the lock on now. Let's do this on our way home tonight. 'Course, the trolls might be out then, and we'd be locking 'em out instead of in."

"You're nuts." he said. "Did you know that?"

"Then explain what happened to Sandra."

He turned paler than he already was. "I can't explain it," he said. "But I'm afraid we'll never see her again."

"Me too."

When me and Walter stopped at the outhouse to put on the lock, I asked him to look for trolls. He refused. Didn't really surprise me none, so I begged. He still said no. The louse.

He said he'd put on the lock so he could get home, but that was it. As he walked to the building, mumbling under his breath, I grabbed the axe I'd bought from Walmart during my supper break. He started working and was using both hands. That's when I walloped him with it. I smashed his skull with just one blow.

Walter'd never actually done nothing to me, *yet*, but I could see it in his eyes. He wanted to. And he'd done something to Sandra. I was sure of it. Well, pretty sure...

I could barely see 'cause the moon hid behind a thick blanket of clouds, and I didn't dare leave my headlights on. I knew I couldn't put him in the portajohn—it weren't deep enough. I pulled him on the tarp down to the river. I chopped him up just like I did my brother, and, piece by piece, threw him as far as I could into the fast moving water. He'd be halfway to the Gulf of Mexico in a day or two. I wrapped the axe in the tarp and slung it in the river, too. I rinsed my hands in some backflow from the river and wiped 'em dry. Another job well done...one less troll to worry about.

When I got through, I put the lock back on myself. I didn't have to worry about human trolls...for now...just the outhouse ones.

THE ICE TREE

Charlee Vale

I N AN ODD LITTLE TOWN on the edge of the mountains, there were only two rules that ever mattered: Don't let the rising sunlight strike you, and never touch the ice tree. Frankly, if you considered everything about the town—from the weeping windows to the screaming library—the tree at the center of town was one of the most normal things in it. At the very least you could say it didn't bother anyone.

Except for Maria Temple.

The tree was beautiful in its own way. It was gnarled and twisted back on itself, stretched out as if running from the wind. But the shape wasn't the first thing people noticed. That was the ice. Half an inch thick—at least—it lay smooth and glassy on every bare bone and branch. The ice had surrounded the tree for as long as anyone in the town could remember.

At least it was pretty. It was the children's constant plaything, no matter the season. Daring each other close as a breath in the winter, and picking the flowers from the perpetual melt in summer.

But nothing compared to the tree at night. Every other mountain town had lights in the sky. Here, the lights were in the tree—swirling and mesmerizing in eddies running through the ice. Lights that pulled you in and made you forget there was such a thing as time. Blues, greens, purples, and a rare gold. They never followed the same path, but rather flowed where they wished, with seeming minds of their own.

Occasionally some visitor to the town would see the tree and, astounded as they always were, spread the word about it. And for a time people would come to look at the tree trapped in ice, the tree that glowed. But with all the visitors, and all the memories, no one had ever known why it existed. No one had ever asked.

The tree sang to Maria Temple from the time she was a girl. On the day the town gathered to celebrate the coming of Spring, she heard a music unlike anything she knew. She followed the sound until she stood face to face with the tree, the ice glassy in the spring heat, the branches shivering with the strange music.

Her family heard her tale, and paid it no mind. Maria was not the first girl in the town to hear a tree singing, and there were worse things that could happen to a child. So Maria grew and listened to the songs the tree would sing to her. She spent days on the grass in the square, hearing the variations and echoes, the years passing without ever hearing the same song twice.

It was Winter, the tree frosted and frozen, when something changed. The air was cold and clear—each exhaled breath forming the shape of a thought—and Maria Temple was walking across the square. It was late, and she was returning home from a party where the young people of the town stayed out as long as they dared. They lingered until the glow of dawn was peeking over the crest of the mountains, risking the rays of the morning sun.

But Maria knew all too well the dangers of the morning light, and the moon was still high when she made her way across the empty square. Her path along the cobblestones took her past the tree of ice, aglow as it always was, and singing. The buildings on the edge of the square were tinged with its changing colors.

Ducking under the branches of the tree, Maria had passed it by when the music stopped. Suddenly she was experiencing a silence she had never felt before, and she was unsure.

Then, "Maria."

It was barely an echo on the wind, but she stilled. She looked around the square—she was alone.

"Maria."

It came from over her shoulder, yet there was no one in sight.

It was considered a good omen to see a golden thread of light weaving through the ice, rare as the sight was. Maria turned to find the whole tree shot through with it. Golden light twisted around the trunk, taking over the other colors and releasing them again. It curved around the icy branches, crawling along each one to its end and glowing brighter. Maria looked beneath her feet and saw that the light was bleeding through the cobblestones, through every root of the tree until the entire tangled system that sprawled under the square stood before her brighter than it had ever been, burning a solid gold.

Maria stood as frozen as the tree, awe and fear binding her to the spot. The tree had been a constant her entire life, never changing. While the gold was a good omen, change was not. This was clearly a mistake. A dream. Tomorrow all would be well.

She was turning to leave when she heard it again. "Maria." A whisper. The voice of a child. "Maria." Another voice, deeper. A man. Then another voice, and another, and another, overlapping each other, rustling like the sound of leaves. Each voice different, and familiar.

The whispers rose like a tide. Each voice saying her name, growing more urgent until Maria could only cover her ears. The sounds rooted her to the ground and pulled at her soul. Then as suddenly as they had started, the voices collapsed into silence. The light in the tree and the roots faded, and Maria cautiously uncovered her ears. Then the tree spoke again—the golden light pulsing with each word, and all thousand voices combined into one.

"Maria," they said. "Help us."

Maria's entire body chilled with fear. The whispers returned, saying her name, pleading for help. The golden light rippled beneath the trunk, and despite herself, Maria was mesmerized. The light was making shapes, and she thought she could see faces that matched the whispers. Faces and hands and remnants of lives.

The burning in her fingers brought her back, and she looked down to see her hand reaching out to the tree, touching the trunk. The cold of the ice was slicing through her fingers, burning and spreading the glow into her own body. Maria ripped her hand away from the cold, pretending she did not see the child-sized hand pressed against the inside of the tree where hers had just been.

The golden light faded more quickly this time, pulsing only a little with the final words. Again, the voice of a child. "Help us."

Then the voice was gone. The ground was solid beneath her feet. The square was dark and so was the tree. She was alone.

Maria turned and ran.

Maria didn't tell anyone about what she had seen that night. It's not that they wouldn't believe her; they would. But she had touched the tree. No one talked about what happened to the people who broke that rule, but Maria knew it had happened before. If she told no one, perhaps no one—not even the gods that presided over the town—would know the rule was broken. But at night she could still see the golden glow staining her fingers, and dread flowed from them to her belly and pooled there in the shadows.

The tree began to sing to her again. Sad and whispering songs meant for melancholy and nothing more. Maria tried to cross the square as little as possible. The little girl's voice appeared in her head every time she passed the tree, asking for help. How could she help? There was nothing to do. Little by little more of her hand took on the remnant of the tree's glow.

Winter passed, and as the Spring came the songs the tree sang returned to what they had been. If anything, they were more beautiful than before. There were no more whispers to hear, and Maria was no longer afraid.

The town prepared to come together for the Spring festival, and the square was filled with flowers and ribbons and other things useless in Winter. The night before the celebration the tree was especially beautiful. Those rare glimpses of gold were seen more than once, and those preparing thought it a sign of a good Spring to come.

Maria was one of the last in the square, tasked by the elders to beautify the town's central hall. It took longer than she had expected, distracted as she had been by the tree's songs. The sun set and the moon rose, and as Maria finished she thought to sit and rest under the tree for a moment.

Her hand was brighter now, but she didn't mind. She matched the tree, which was sprouting its veins of gold and melting into brightness. Maria thought she might be afraid to be alone with the tree again, but dismissed the feeling. That strange night was so long ago now. Nothing else had gone wrong. The world was beautiful, and the voices were singing to her.

Maria wondered why she had ever thought there was anything that mattered other than this light and this sound. Her hands found the trunk, slippery and cold, burning her palms. Maria's eyes grew heavy with comfort as the voices sang a chorus of her name in her mind. She wasn't sure when the song had turned into words, but she wished that it had always been so.

The ice was no longer frosted and the images dancing in the tree were ones she wanted to see closer. She let her body lean against the tree, the cold of the ice both painful and wonderful. She could stay like this forever. If only she could hear this music for a lifetime. She sat, hugging the tree close, and let the song and light drench her mind. She closed her eyes.

Maria felt herself being drawn away, drawn inward. The music swelled, and she didn't open her eyes. She never wanted to again. The song turned sharper, and something inside her let go. She tried to turn back, but the tide of the song was too much. She was being pulled further and further away.

Then she could hear that the voices were not singing. They were screaming. She couldn't open her eyes.

When she could see again, it was quiet. Maria found that she was looking in a mirror. The mirror was warped and showed her face from an odd angle—one she'd never seen before. She reached out to touch her reflection and found nothing. Something brushed by her and she shifted, but could not turn. What she saw was nothing, and everything. Faces and hands and remnants of lives. A thousand bodies passed through her, a thousand voices ringing through ears that are no longer there.

She heard a scream, but muffled, on the outside. In the square where the town awaited to celebrate Spring, there was now a crowd. Now there was mourning. The faceless faces gathered around Maria and watched the scene with interest.

Maria stared at her body on the ground, watched as people gathered for yet another strange funeral in a tiny town. She screamed. She screamed and screamed and her voice was endless and effortless in this place. A little girl with brown eyes turned toward the tree and smiled. Maria knew the music she heard, but she could not speak a warning.

Because now that she had started to scream she could not stop. The rest of the faces screamed with her. Her voice blended in with the other thousand, waiting for the day when the little girl would give in and touch the ice.

We will make her touch the ice. Perhaps one day she'll know what to do. Perhaps she'll set us free. Or maybe she'll join us. We scream.

Lost

Matt Sinclair

"Let me pass you over to your son." Then there was a pause. I hear a whisper.

"Hello?"

"Kevin," I say, "I need to get home."

"Where are you?"

"I'm…" where am I? "I'm in…" I'm not sure. Where is this? It looks familiar. "I'm near the church."

"Are you in your apartment?"

"Yes. But I need to get home."

"Where is home?" What a ridiculous question. How could he not know where home is? "On Man…" wait "on Man…" something isn't right "on Man…"

"Manor View?" he asks. He knows what I'm talking about.

"Yes, Manor View"

"Mom, you sold that house twenty years ago."

Wait. There's something familiar about… Wait, when… "Oh."

"You live in the apartment, Mom. That's your apartment"

This cannot be. "But I need to get home."

"You are home. You live in that apartment."

"But…" is this real? "But there's no one here."

"I know, Mom." He sighs. What does that mean? "You live alone now."

"Oh." The coldness of my bed occurs to me. The loneliness. The way even soft noises can wake me. "Can't I go home?"

"Not to the house on Manor View," he says. "I don't even know who lives there these days."

These days. It has been years. And how long is it since Henry passed? "Well, what am I supposed to do?"

"What room are you in, Mom?"

"I'm in the kitchen."

"On the microwave, what time does it say?"

I look. "11:57."

"Yes, it's almost midnight," he says. "I recommend you go to bed."

I never liked sleeping in a strange place. "Well, perhaps that's for the best."

"After a good night's sleep," he says, "you hopefully will have a clearer picture."

"What do I do?"

He is silent for a moment. "What do you mean?"

"I mean what do I do tomorrow."

"Well, what do you usually do on a Wednesday?"

Tomorrow is Wednesday. I thought it was Monday. "Well, on Wednesdays, I usually go to church."

"Does Mary pick you up?"

Mary who? Oh, yes, Mary! "Yes. Mary will take me to church on Wednesday."

"I can't stop by after work tomorrow, but I will see you on Thursday. All right?"

"Yes. Thursday."

Once more, he says nothing for a moment. "Are you all right for now, Mom?"

The kitchen table is awash with paper. How have I let things get so disorganized? "I guess."

"You're going to bed? It's midnight."

"Yes. I think I'll go to bed."

"Ok, I'll call you tomorrow from the office."

"All right. Thank you." I know he will. Something tells me he does that every day, but I can't be quite sure.

"I love you, Mom."

I smile. That was familiar, at least. "I love you too."

We hang up. The apartment feels damp. Perhaps a storm is coming. I need to get into my bed clothes. … Oh, wait. I am already. Was I in bed? What woke me up?

"Henry? Are you awake? I'm coming to bed."

I stand and walk to the empty bedroom. My bed seems small. And lonely. I turn off the bedroom light and walk gingerly in the dark. The red light of the digital clock reads 12:02. So dark outside, despite the lamps along the path. I'm not very tired, but perhaps I should get some sleep.

The bed is comfortable, the sheets clean. I think I hear the voice of Henry, who has been dead for at least five years now. "Is that you, Henry?"

No, it's someone in the apartment upstairs. I hear feet moving above me. How big is this building?

I close my eyes. "Dorothy," Henry says. "It won't be long now." And I smile.

Acknowledgements

The latest anthology has been a labor of love for me, which might seem ironic given the nature of the stories inside. But I've always loved a good scare—almost as much as I love working with talented, creative people.

I want to thank all the writers who spun their spooky and intense yarns and shared them with us. I offer a special thank you to Mindy McGinnis, who remains a valuable contributor not only of wonderful stories but also of her opinions and perspective. I don't want to get maudlin in my praise of her and her writing, but I don't think anyone will be surprised when I say I own or will own a copy of every book she's authored. I also want to thank MarcyKate Connolly, author of the wonderful middle-grade story *Monstrous*, who also provided wise and regular counsel throughout the long process of putting together a new anthology.

A special thank you to Charlee Hoffman, who once again produced a stunning cover for us. And I remain thoroughly indebted to R.C. Lewis, who agreed once again to serve as book designer, even as she was promoting her latest novel, the intriguing *Spinning Starlight*, and teaching math to dozens of fortunate youth in Utah.

About the Authors

E.B. Black is the annoying writer who lives in the head of an average, nerdy housewife named Elizabeth. Elizabeth tries to live out her days walking her dogs, doing housework, and watching television, but E.B. Black makes her drop everything and type out weird fantasy stories, disrupting her life. Elizabeth is asking anyone who reads this to please send help and not read any of E.B. Black's books—it just encourages her.

When not writing, **Kay Elam** can usually be found curled up with a good book or creating the homemade organic hair and beauty products sprinkled throughout her Music City Mystery series. She is represented by Paula Munier of the Talcott Notch Literary Agency. Kay enjoys yoga and her back porch, where she meditates and watches her flowers grow—though not necessarily at the same time. She lives outside Nashville, Tennessee, with her husband, Greg.

Kim Graff writes creepy, weird, and sinister YA. Aside from having an obsession with all things books and publishing, she enjoys traveling and has lived in Australia, France, and Quebec. Currently, she resides in New York City where she balances her time between drinking copious amounts of coffee and wine and writing her next novel.

Justin Holley is the author of the novel *Bruised* and several short stories published in magazines and anthologies around the world. He also investigates the paranormal with a TAPS-family group and plays volleyball twice a week. Correspondence from his fans is encouraged, and the best way to contact him is through his website, www.justinholley.com.

Precy Larkins grew up in the Philippines where superstitions ran rampant and tales of *aswang*, or ghouls, invaded her bedtime stories. But it was the abandoned house next door that would fill her nighttime musings. She lives in Utah now with her husband and three children (no haunted mansions nearby). She writes YA fiction and is represented by Julia A. Weber. Her short stories have previously appeared in anthologies published by Elephant's Bookshelf Press. You can visit her online at precylarkins.wordpress.com.

Sarah Glenn Marsh writes young adult novels and children's picture books. She lives in Virginia with her husband and four rescued greyhounds, and when she's not writing, she's often engaged in pursuits of the nerd variety from video games to tabletop adventures and dungeon crawls. Her work is represented by Christa Heschke of McIntosh and Otis. Her YA historical fantasy, *Fear the Drowning Deep*, debuts with Sky Pony in September of 2016. Visit her online at www.sarahglennmarsh.com.

Mindy McGinnis is a YA author who has worked in a high school library for thirteen years. Her debut, *Not a Drop to Drink*, a post-apocalyptic survival story set in a world with very little freshwater, has been optioned for film by Stephenie Meyer's Fickle Fish Films. The companion novel, *In a Handful of Dust*, was released in 2014, and her Gothic historical thriller, *A Madness So Discreet* released in October of 2015 from Katherine Tegen Books. Mindy is represented by Adriann Ranta of Wolf Literary.

R.S. Mellette is a proud member of the Elephant's Bookshelf herd. Besides short stories in five of its seven anthologies, Mellette authored EBP's 2014 novel, *Billy Bobble Makes a Magic Wand*. Look for the sequel, *Billy Bobble and the Witch Hunt*, coming soon. Outside of EBP, Mellette wrote the first web-to-television intellectual property, "The Xena Scrolls," for Universal Studio's *Xena: Warrior Princess*. He also has had various jobs from script coordinator to actor on *Blue Crush*, *Nutty Professor II*, *Looney Tunes: Back In Action*, *Star Trek: Enterprise*, *Days of Our Lives*, *Too Young The Hero*, and countless stage productions across the U.S.

Madeline Mora-Summonte is a writer and a reader, a beach-comber and a tortoise-owner. Her work appears in many publications, both online and in print, including *Hint Fiction: An Anthology of Stories in 25 Words or Fewer* (W.W. Norton, 2011.) She is the author the flash fiction collections, *The People We Used to Be* and *Garden of Lost Souls*. Please visit her online at www.MadelineMora-Summonte.com.

Matt Sinclair is a New York City-based journalist covering philanthropy and charity and a freelance editor and writer covering as much of everything else as he can. He blogs at the Elephant's Bookshelf and helped create the From the Write Angle blog. He tweets from @Elephantguy68. In 2012, he established Elephant's Bookshelf Press, LLC, which has now published ten books including the novel *Billy Bobble Makes a Magic Wand* by R.S. Mellette and the anti-bullying anthology *Tales from the Bully Box*.

A.M. Supinger writes an eclectic mix of fantasy, horror, and erotic romance. Although A.M. is a fan of happily-ever-afters, her own work tends to be dark; most peels away humanity and looks at the epic rot within. For a peek at her somewhat random thoughts, check out @AMSupinger on Twitter.

Charlee Vale is a photographer, writer, and overall artsy person living in New York City. She can usually be found in the vicinity of a bookstore, adding to the list of books she'll never finish reading. Also, she loves tea.